OUTLAW NO MORE

Now, I can be about as dumb as anybody. But it didn't take me extra long to work out in my mind that I didn't really want anybody here in this town to know that I wasn't some marshal named Tanner.

There was only one thing that I knew for absolute certain sure about this Tanner fellow. And that was that the man was dead.

It seemed pretty likely that I was the only person who did know that he was dead.

And I didn't want anybody coming to the conclusion that I was the fellow who'd gone and made him dead.

I mean, here I was, wandering around with his horse and saddle and credentials—and his money in hand, and him laying out there dead on the hard, cold ground somewhere north of town.

If it came out that I wasn't him . . . and that the real Marshal Tanner was cold meat . . . well, I wouldn't hardly blame folks for jumping to the obvious conclusions. . . .

OUTLAW
WITH A STAR

Dave Austin

BERKLEY BOOKS, NEW YORK

OUTLAW WITH A STAR

A Berkley Book / published by arrangement with
the author

PRINTING HISTORY
Berkley edition / April 1999

ISBN: 0-425-16817-4

BERKLEY®
Berkley Books are published by The Berkley Publishing Group,
a member of Penguin Putnam Inc.,
375 Hudson Street, New York, New York 10014.
BERKLEY and the "B" logo
are trademarks belonging to Berkley Publishing Corporation.

PRINTED IN THE UNITED STATES OF AMERICA

10 9 8 7 6 5 4 3 2 1

For my friend and saddle pard—okay, so it's a pickup truck and not a saddle—Bernie Nalaboff

OUTLAW
WITH A STAR

ONE

Go south, they said. Warm nights and hot señoritas, they said. Texas is the place to winter, they said.

They lied.

I tried to hunker even deeper into the coat and made a vain attempt to tug the collar higher. I already had my spare shirt wrapped around my ears and last week's socks pulled over my hands, and still all the extremities were lost and gone so far as sensation was concerned. All the pointy parts were numb by now. Which probably should have been a blessing but was not due to my worry that something could have dropped off by now entirely unnoticed.

The lone ray of sunshine, so to speak, was that if I did have to go back and look for something, a nose or an ear or whatever, it should be easy enough to find as the wind that made me so miserable was dry and empty of snow. I wouldn't have thought it possible to be so thoroughly bone-deep cold without there being so much as a wee threat of snow, except it was true. The sky above me was a bright and mockingly cheerful blue bowl from one horizon to the next.

I grumbled and muttered and shifted from one stirrup to the other trying to keep some feeling in my feet, but about all that accomplished was to peeve my horse. The ugly brown creature shook its head angrily and laid its ears flat.

I didn't blame it. It wasn't used to such abuse, but then neither was I. And anyway how do you explain things to a dumb brute.

The wind picked up speed and cut even deeper, and I had to grab my hat to keep from having to watch it sail off toward Mexico without me.

As best I could determine this wind was whistling down straight out of Canada, and the only thing between me and the border was two strands of bob wire somewhere up in Kansas. And from the feel of things, one of those strings had gone and fallen down.

"Carry me to a windbreak, ugly, and we'll take us a break from all the fun we're having," I mumbled as best I could between lips that were cracked and about half frozen.

The horse didn't twitch, just kept plodding along with its rump to the wind and its tail tucked in tight. If I'd had a tail, I would've tucked it in close too.

Not for the first time I had second thoughts about this trip. Maybe I should have stayed. Maybe I should have . . .

No, danggit. I shouldn't have stayed. More to the point, I couldn't have. It was too hot back home in Kansas—different sort of heat, of course—and lately even my old run-to spots down in the Indian Territories couldn't be relied on anymore.

What it came down to was that I'd just about used up all the possibilities back home and in all the easy-to-reach places too.

Too many people knew me back there. And way too many of them were subject to the temptations of greed. It would have been just too dang easy for one of them, any unexpected soul among them, to pick up some easy money by tipping John Law to me.

It was with that unpleasant prospect behind me that I was making this little trip south for the winter.

I thought about stuff like that, ruing the twists and turns of fortune that'd brought me to this low state, and buried my discomfort under a blanket of self-pity while ugly carried me along at a shambling, stiff-legged gait that told me as good as words could have done that he was feeling about as resentful as I was.

But then maybe ugly had some sense of the trouble that was waiting down south. Me, I didn't have a clue. Good thing too or I would've turned smack around and ridden north into the teeth of that bitter cold wind and never mind the consequences. Hey, they provide heat in jail cells, don't they? Reckon I should have thought of that while I still had the chance.

TWO

It was late afternoon before I found a spot worth stopping at. I crossed into a flat depression, not anywhere near deep enough to be considered a valley, but a wide place where once in a while a creek must have run. There was a pale, meandering streak of sand out in the middle of things to show that water ran there sometimes, most likely in the spring of the year when rain and snowmelt would combine to make more live water than the ground could soak up. Most of the time, of course, now included, the broad, flat bed was as dried up and useless as a whore's heart.

That didn't impress me much, but off to my right, to the west of where I came onto the drainage, I could see a hump in the ground that was maybe twenty, thirty feet taller than the surrounding prairie. It was caused by a deposit of hard rock that hadn't weathered or washed away like everything around it.

You could see where over the years some parts of the stone had chunked off and fallen away from the main deposit so there was a sort of undersized cliff on the north side and at the base of this stony hump a scattering of boulders. There were a dozen or so of these boulders, ranging in size, I'd say, from about that of a pony cart on up to a good-sized farm wagon.

With that kind of windbreak at my back there was a

chance I might yet live out this blow without freezing to death.

And, all right I admit it, I was pleased as well to see that I could snug down inside that nest of boulders there, me and ugly both, and not be seen from afar.

That sort of thinking, I supposed, had become pretty much of a habit with me, and I just naturally felt better when I wasn't on display, just the same as I always feel more comfortable in a room full of strangers when I have my back to a wall or at the very least have a backbar mirror I can look into to make sure there isn't anybody lurking around behind me.

Like I say, this wasn't all that important to me at the moment, for as far as I knew there was no reason why anyone in Texas should take any interest in me. I wasn't wanted for anything here, and there wasn't any reason why anyone south of the Indian Territories should ever have heard my name.

Still and all, caution is a sensible thing and was a habit drilled into me by years of necessity.

I guided ugly to the west, toward that rocky hump in the ground, making him more than a little bit mad because that put him sideways to the direction of the wind and made us both that much colder for the added exposure.

To compensate for that just a little, and because I knew he wouldn't be asked to keep on spending the energy very long, I bumped the horse into an easy lope, not so much effort as to bring up a sweat that would chill him when it froze on him afterward, but enough of a workout that it should warm his muscles a bit.

We got to the rocks in ten, fifteen minutes or so, and I think ugly was as pleased as me when we slid down inside the protection of that rock face. I could hear the wind moan and cuss about losing its prey, but the sound of it was overhead where it could do no harm. I went in between the face and the fallen boulders, and that provided plenty enough of a south-side windbreak to stop any of the little eddies of swirling wind that might curl back toward us.

I hobbled ugly, carried my kak to a soft-looking spot

close to the base of the rock face and turned the horse loose. There were a few wisps of old grass sprouting here and there that he could chew on if he wanted, and anyway he wasn't likely to wander out into the cold again unless I forced him into it.

A fire would have made the setup the next thing to home-like, but there wasn't anything flammable anywhere in sight, this particular stretch of country running somewhat short on firewood. And trees. And very much of anything else that stood taller than a man's boot tops.

I didn't even bother considering going out into that wind again to look for old buffalo chips or whatever else might burn. Maybe come tomorrow, but right at that point in time I wasn't much in the mood.

The truth is that right at that particular moment, I wasn't much in the mood for very much of anything save brooding and self-pity.

Self-pity is not what you might call a particularly en-dearing trait in a man, and generally I frown on it. On the other hand I've been known to plead guilty to it now and then.

Would have to plead guilty to certain other things too, of course, which is perhaps the biggest reason why I was enjoying my wallow in the cesspool of self-pity just then.

I mean, when I was a kid I never laid awake at night thinking, gosh almighty gee, when I grow up I wanta be a hungry, hunted, shivering cold outcast outlaw with a price on my head and no hope for any sort of decent future.

But that's what it had come down to, and I hardly even knew how it had gone and happened.

It just sort of did.

And now here I was, bone-deep miserable, in a place far from what passed for a home—not that I had an actual home to yearn for—and with no real hope that any part of it would ever change for the better.

I made sure ugly was comfortable, then settled down where I was well out of the wind but could keep an eye out across the brown stubble of last spring's grass and make sure nobody crept up on me unawares. I wrapped my saddle blanket tight around my ears and sat there peering out on a world that was as cold and bleak as my prospects. What all I saw wasn't pretty, not when I was looking out, and even less so when I was staring inward.

THREE

There was a fairly sharp rise in the ground about a mile, mile and a quarter to the south of my wind-proof nest of rocks. I hadn't known that until a rider came busting over the top of it and into my line of sight.

The man was riding belly down and hell-for-leather, crouched low over the withers of his horse and quirting the animal hard.

Even from that far off I could see that he'd better get to where he was going pretty dang soon if he wanted to do it ahorseback, because that animal was about wore out. It wasn't going to take him much further without a rubdown and a serious amount of rest.

The horse was paddling with its forefeet, sort of flopping them out in front of its stride as fatigue sapped its balance and control.

I felt a rush of anger then. Men can be sons of bitches and a goodly many of them I haven't had any use for, but horses are honest. I've never had one lie to me or give me anything but the best it had to offer, and nobody ought to treat a horse like this man was.

The fellow looked like he was headed for the shelter of this same hole-up where I already was, and I hoped that was true for I wanted to have me some words with anyone who would so mistreat an animal.

Then I saw why it was the man was larruping his mount in such a big hurry, and I had to take back the unkind thoughts I'd just then been thinking. He had a better than merely average reason for running like that.

The guy was about halfway from the crest of the far rise out to the creek bed when three more horsebackers popped into view and all of them running just as hard in pursuit of the first guy.

Three-to-one odds are a mite long to draw to, and I forgave him for asking so much of the horse.

The three doing the chasing were on horses that were about as worn out as the first one was. They were quirting and hollering and waving rifles in the air as they rode, and I couldn't help but root for the lone guy out in front of this parade.

Far as this affair was concerned I didn't know gee from haw, but I just naturally had to take sides with the one that was being chased. After all, that was a position I'd found myself in a right good many times in the past. I didn't know doo-squat about what it was like to be the one doing the chasing and would have had a little trouble working up a sympathetic feel to the thing.

I blinked a few times and sat up a little taller then, when it came to me that I might well have to take one side or the other if these boys kept on in the direction they were traveling. If the man on the run got into this bunch of rocks, where none of them could know I already was, there was apt to be some shooting going on. And I'd had plenty enough troubles at the hands of men with guns before. I hadn't wanted any of them to take me down, even if they more or less had the right to, and it would have been even more insulting now for a bunch of strangers to do it by accident.

I sighed and mumbled and grumbled just a little. And reached for the saddle carbine that habit had prompted me to put close to hand when I sat down here.

The guy who was doing the running reached the soft sand of the creek bed, and his already flagging horse slowed down as the depth of the sand added to its misery. That let the other three, who were still running on hard ground, close the gap between them. Two of the chasers kept coming on hard, but one of them had the presence of mind—not that I approved, you understand, but I was forced to admire the move in what you might call a professional sort of way—presence of mind enough to swing out to the side a little way so as to give himself a clear line of sight that avoided his partners.

He swung off to the right just a little, threw himself off his horse and steadied himself for a rifle shot at the man out front.

I could see the puff of smoke from the muzzle of the rifle and then quickly another, meaning he had himself a repeater. There was no way I could see where his shots flew, and the sound of them never reached me, being as the wind was blowing from my back toward the source of the noise.

The man out in front reached hard ground on my side of the creek bed, and his horse lunged gamely if awkwardly ahead. Out behind him the man on the ground fired three more times, but the distance was pretty far by then and I doubt the shots could have had much effect, especially since one of those I did happen to see, when it kicked up a small plume of dust a good eighty or a hundred yards back of the rider he was shooting at.

The other two kept coming hard, but their horses were as tired as the one the first guy was riding and they weren't able to close on him again after they had to ride through the creek bed, and the separation increased to what it had been before or maybe a little more.

The fellow on the gray horse—they were close enough I could make out more details now—was naturally enough heading straight for my bunch of protective rocks. Well, I couldn't blame him. The stone would give protection from lead as well as it did from wind, and it's where I'd have wanted to be too if I was in his saddle.

The guy came as hard as his horse could go, and within moments he was close enough that I could hear the tired, choppy gait of his poor, worn-out horse and could see him hunched low to his saddle, looking behind him at the men who were bent on killing him, leaving his reins slack and

letting the horse find its own way those last few rods into
the nest of boulders.

It seemed more than a trifle off that he would let the
horse go unguided. But then he knew his animal better than
I could, so who was I to criticize.

The horse came gasping and trembling into the rocks, its
forequarters slick with sweat that steamed in the cold like
smoke pouring off a green-wood fire.

I grabbed the horse's bit and pulled it to a stop. Its legs
were quivering so hard I thought for a moment it might
fall.

I looked up into the pale, drawn face of the man who'd
just chosen to join me and saw why he'd dropped his reins
out there. Something else had come up that was of more
interest to him at the time, you might say.

The guy's coat was open, and his shirt was drenched with
blood. At least one of the bullets from those men out there
had taken him in the back and plowed right on through to
come out the front of him in the neighborhood of his col-
larbone. He'd already lost more blood than you might think
one lone human person would have in him, and more was
leaking out even as I stared.

The man was still alive, though. He looked down at me.
His mouth opened like as if he wanted to say something.
Then both his mouth and his eyes drooped shut, and he
toppled sideways off his saddle.

I caught him. Never took time to think about it but just
naturally did it and eased him down to the ground.

I looked out toward where the riders were still coming
on, two of them out in front now and the third lagging a
couple hundred yards back.

There wasn't time to do much in the way of analytical
thinking and anyway I suppose I'd have come to the same
conclusion even if I'd had until next Tuesday to think on
it. This guy was being chased, and those guys were doing
the chasing, and my sympathies just naturally lay with the
guy who was the object of the manhunt.

My carbine was still in my hand and without bothering to worry about who was who or what was going on, I stepped over to one of the nearby boulders, used it as a rest for my barrel and took a calm, deliberate, careful aim.

FOUR

It would have been easy to knock at least one of those boys out of the saddle quick before the other one had time to turn around and run out of range, but it has been my experience that shooting people tends to make them mad. Or at least it pretty thoroughly peeves the survivors and any of their friends. I chose a spot underneath the belly of the nearer rider's horse—in tight enough that a ricochet wasn't likely to hit the horse—and touched one off. An entirely satisfactory spray of sand and gravel stung hell out of the animal's lower legs, and its rider found himself in the middle of a storm. The guy lost his reins, grabbed horn with both hands and became a passenger on a runaway train while the horse spun around and made for home in a hurry.

The other rider took a long look at the boulders where I was hidden. I suspect the possibilities didn't look what you would call extra attractive. Those guys out there wouldn't know there were two men inside the nest of rocks. But then they didn't have to. It was already plain enough to them that there was a man with a rifle inside the protection, a rifle and a solid rest to shoot it from.

Three men, assuming the runaway managed to get hold of his reins again before Sunday, charging horseback across bare, open ground against a hidden fellow with a repeating rifle is not the sort of odds even a desperate gambler wants to draw to. It didn't come as any surprise to me at all when the one fellow close to me reined back around and went the other way.

He paused to explain the situation to the one who'd fallen behind and the two of them went back south more or less in the direction their runaway pal had just disappeared to over that far rise. They knew they were way out of rifle range by then, of course, so they gave their horses a break and held the pace to an easy road jog.

Which left me alone now in the thin, pale light of late afternoon with a wounded man.

I waited to make sure those boys out there didn't have something tricky on their minds. It would have been easy enough for them to ride out of sight, then swing wide and come around behind the hump of rock at my back. I doubted they would do that, though. For one thing they had no way to know that their quarry was down and bleeding. All they would have seen was the man's mount disappearing into the rocks. It was after that that he fell out of the saddle, and even if they'd seen that from a distance, it just would have looked like he was jumping down to come shoot at them. Which I'd gone and done in his place. Once they were out of sight, the chasers would have to assume that their prey would mount up and skedaddle, so I figured I was safe enough right here where I was.

If that proved to be wrong, well, we'd just look to that if and when it happened, that's all. Right at the moment there was a wounded man for me to see to, and I didn't for a minute think there was any chance he was feeling up to crawling onto a horse again and covering ground.

I leaned my carbine up against a handy chunk of rock and knelt beside the wounded guy.

He was bloody from his throat to his waist, sopping wet with the stuff. The fresher blood from up near his neck steamed in the cold air as bad as his horse's sweat. Smelled bad too. I've always hated the new-penny smell of blood. My own in particular. I pressed the back of my hand to the guy's forehead. He felt dang near as cold as the boulder I'd been leaning against a minute earlier.

The man must've felt my touch. He opened his eyes and peered up at me for five, six long seconds.

Then the funniest dang thing happened. Not the laughing sort of funny, of course, but the odd kind. This fellow's eyes went wide and for a moment there I would've thought he knew me or something. His mouth opened and he tried to say something, I'll never know what, then he coughed and began to choke.

The spasm of coughing lasted only a few seconds and was replaced by a red, frothy bubble of blood that spilled out over his lips and down one side of his cheek.

His eyes were still aware at that point, and I think he knew he was dying. Even so he gave me this odd, curious look.

And then he was gone.

It was a shame, I'm sure. Somewhere he likely had folks that cared about him. But I didn't know the man or what his troubles had been, and his passing really shouldn't have mattered much to me.

For some reason that I couldn't put a handle to, though, I felt bothered by this fellow's troubles.

I didn't know him, nor could he've known me. But dang-git, I sure felt like I did somehow or like I ought to know him. Like I recognized him even though I'd never in my life before seen him.

It bothered me and I thought about it for a spell while I went and rummaged through my saddlebags for something I could eat without having to go out into the wind looking for the means to make a fire. I found a small and shriveledy little potato and munched on that, peel and all, and wished for a pot of steaming hot coffee to wash it down with.

All the while, though, I kept thinking about that dead man, wondering what it was about him that was bothering me so. After a bit I went back to where he was lying and got down beside him again.

His skin was yellow and waxy-looking in death, and the stubble of a couple days' growth of beard on his face was in stark contrast to the pallor of his flesh.

Apart from that though he looked . . . I frowned a little

at the thought and decided no, that couldn't possibly be. No dang way.

I leaned closer and looked again. Took the guy's hat away. Went around to the other side of the body and stared.

Jesus! No wonder he'd given me that wild-eyed look when he was dying. He'd seen it before I did. No wonder it scared him.

The face I was looking at now, the face he'd been looking at then, was one I'd dang sure seen before.

Every time I'd looked into a mirror my whole life long.

This man looked enough like me we could've been twin brothers. Hell, this man looked enough like me that he could've *been* me.

It was like I was looking at myself lying dead on the cold ground there. What this poor SOB must've thought, knowing he was dying and looking up at like his own ghost, that I couldn't hardly imagine, and it's a darn shame I couldn't ask him about it now.

I felt . . . really odd once I realized how awful much the same we looked. Really odd and not right at that moment prepared to do any serious thinking about it.

I grabbed his hat from where I'd laid it a moment before and set it over top of his face so I wouldn't have to see again. Then I went over to where his horse had stopped beside mine, pulled the dead man's gear off of it and tore a handful of dry grass up so I could use that to commence giving the worn-out animal a rubdown. Having something to do like that sure beat moping around and thinking how it so easy could've been me laid out dead on a cold and blowy afternoon.

It was the sort of discovery that got a man to thinking in spite of himself, and these were not thoughts that I really wanted to entertain. So I concentrated on taking care of the horse and let it go at that for the time being.

FIVE

The night that followed was, I think, the longest I've ever my whole life spent. It would have been unpleasant enough what with the cold and no fire and being hungry. What made it worse was that I was as cold inside right then as I was on the outside.

The dead man had a nice thick sougan tied in a fat roll behind his saddle, and I took that and laid it out inside the protection of the boulders and crawled inside it, but even that wasn't enough to make me comfortable enough to get any sleep. I laid awake just about the night long, thinking and wondering.

Thinking about the past. Wondering about the future.

Thinking about how I'd come to this lousy state. Wondering if I so much as had a future.

The point kept coming back to me through that long, nasty night that so far I hadn't accomplished a lot in this life I was leading.

I think I've already mentioned that I hadn't exactly chosen the life I was living. It just kind of snuck up on me without me hardly noticing until it was too late to change anything.

I'd started out just skylarking. I hadn't meant to be mean, not ever. Just kind of . . . playful. Out for some giggles and a good time.

The first thing I ever did wrong was when I was in school. I was . . . it took me a minute to think back that far . . . fifteen then, I think. Not more than that and I don't think any younger either. I only meant to show off, you understand. There was a girl, Margaret Anne her name was, in the grade back of me. She had what they used to call cats, rats and mice, that being her hair arranged in two big soft curls and two littler ones and then two tiny wee ones. Blond hair it was, yellow as gold. She was plump and pretty, with dimples on her cheeks and eyelashes as long and curly as a calf's. I can't recall any longer the color of her eyes, but I remember plain as can be that I thought she was the nicest looking filly west of Boston or east of San Francisco, and I would've swapped my soul for a good look at her limbs. In a way you could say that I did turn in my soul for her. But I never did get a peek at her ankles. Reckon I was cheated about that.

What happened was that come Christmas there was this affair at the school with all the pupils taking part, the little ones in costumes and the older kids singing carols and all that kind of thing. Now, I can't sing a lick and never could so what I was supposed to do was tend to the carbide lamps and the colored gels over the light reflectors and move decorations and stuff like that. Heck, it was all such simple stuff that even I couldn't mess it up, clumsy and awkward though I was at that age.

Well, I messed it up anyhow. I wanted to do something to draw attention to myself so Margaret Anne would notice me apart from the rest of the herd.

I spent two whole weeks planning a speech I was gonna jump out and make unannounced when Margaret Anne was through singing her solo song. I even memorized a little poem that went along with it. It's kind of a good thing in a way that my plan didn't quite come off because I would've been humiliated for life if it had. I mean, this deal would've been maudlin.

What happened instead was that I got scared the evening of the pageant and had me a nip of Dutch courage to keep from losing my nerve. And then another nip. And next thing anybody knew I was drunk as a lord. Saw Margaret

Anne in front of the crowd, which included pretty much everybody who lived within a radius of twenty, thirty miles, and went out to her, before she could sing the first note. Went out in front of everybody, got sick to my stomach and puked up all over the front of Margaret Anne's new Christmas dress.

Did I get that girl to notice me? I expect I did so.

Also got myself kicked out of the school, which I now admit was the right and proper thing for them to do. At the time, though, I thought it mighty cruel and wanted me some revenge on the schoolmaster.

His name was Berry. Harold T. Berry. I'll never forget him. I wanted to pay Mr. Berry back for making my life miserable, never mind that I was the one who'd humiliated myself and he hadn't had aught to do with it.

What I did then, being more stupid than most at that age, was decide I'd show him a thing or two. And since everybody knew what a tightwad Mr. Berry was, I figured the way to hurt him the most was to take his money from him.

I waited until he collected his month's pay, then held him up at gunpoint and took all his money away from him.

Fifteen dollars and eighty-three cents. I'll remember that amount until the day I die. That was what Mr. Berry had in his pockets to show for a month's work.

God only knows how much I've stole from others since that time, but the amount I remember best is Mr. Berry's lousy $15.83.

Now, I swear what I wanted was to get back at Mr. Berry for kicking me out of school. I suppose I just plain hadn't thought all the way through what sort of effect my stupid trick would have beyond making Mr. Berry hurt.

Never crossed my mind that he would complain to the town marshal or that the county sheriff would take a hand or that a grand jury would return an indictment against me for armed robbery. Which of course is exactly what happened. Slam, bam and I was wanted.

Now let me tell you how damn dumb kids can be. Okay then, how dumb I was in particular if not kids in general.

I resented Mr. Berry and the grand jurors and the marshal

and the sheriff and all the rest of the good folks around my homeplace.

Heck, I knew it wasn't really much of an armed robbery. My stickup weapon was a piece of junk I picked up off the trash heap out east of town. The old gun was busted and the barrel plugged with mud and whatever. The grips were broken completely off, and the spring had snapped. I had to scrub the rust off with sand for the better part of a day just to make the old thing look menacing.

Well, I expect it was menacing enough to scare Mr. Berry with, all right. And to get me wanted by the law on a charge I still didn't see fit the deed I'd done.

So instead of being sensible when I heard about the warrant against me, instead of taking that junk gun and carrying it to the marshal's office for a confession and a return of Mr. Berry's money, brilliant me, I used most of my first loot to buy me a real gun and two boxes of cartridges, then hitched a ride west on a passing wagon.

I've been on the run ever since. Seventeen years of it.

And God, I've come to wish I hadn't been so awful stupid when I was fifteen years old.

SIX

Things looked some better come the daylight. It's funny the way that always seems to be so. You have a lousy night, cold and hungry and full of gloomy thoughts until it feels like life's deck is stacked against you. Then the sun comes up and brightens the way you feel inside just as much as it brightens the world around you.

I suppose a deep thinker could make something out of that, a preacher, say, or one of those kind of folks. Me, I'm not that smart; I just know what I feel and never mind the rest of it.

Point is, I felt a whole heap better once the tip of the sun poked above the horizon off to my left. Oh, I wasn't a lick warmer. There wasn't light enough in that speck of sun to warm a tub of butter much less the wide, windy prairie here. I knew that. But somehow I *felt* warmer even knowing it wasn't so. Warmer and in a better frame of mind.

And what the heck. Why not? If there were places, even a fair good many of them, where there was a price on my head, it was just as true that I didn't happen to be any of those places right now. They were all behind me. I wasn't wanted for a dang thing in Texas.

Of course there were some folks who thought of Texas as being a part of the United States. Most people up in Kansas and Missoura and the Indian Territories might dis-

agree with that assessment, but I think a majority of people
in the country would concede, however grudgingly, that
Texas was one of the united states.

And that being true, a stray wanted poster might could
find its way south. Warrants from up north could be served
down here too. So I might be far from the seat of my recent
troubles, but that was not to say that I was free of them.
Not entirely.

I sighed and gave a mite of thought to Mexico. They say
once a man gets across the border into another country he's
free for sure. It was something to consider.

Of course they also say there's a whole lot of Mexicans
down in Mexico. I've not had all that much experience with
them, but I've heard tell they mostly don't speak English
like civilized folk always do. And I don't speak a word of
Mexican. I don't think I'd like being in a place where people could say nasty things to my face and me never have
a clue what they were up to. That, and fretting about were
they doing that or not, was the sort of thing that could lead
to some real serious argument of the type best settled with
a club or a knife or a gun. I know myself well enough to
accept truth, and the truth is that I'm not the sort of person
to accept a slight or an insult. Nor even a suspicion of one.
I'd be like to find myself a peck of trouble if I thought
some bunch of bean-eaters were talking light about me.

Anyway, none of the night's worries looked all that
gloomy to me now that it was daylight again, and all my
decisions could be made some other time. They didn't all
have to come in a lump right at this place and time.

I stood up and stretched and tried stomping some feeling
back into my feet. Hadn't taken my boots off overnight, of
course, lest they freeze solid. That would have been annoying.

My belly was rumbling. As if I needed another reminder
of how hungry I was. Now that my favorite potato was
gone, there wasn't anything more in my saddlebags that
could be eaten without cooking, so I pulled the dead guy's
sougan around me like a lighter and fluffier buffalo robe
and headed off with the idea of seeing could I find something on the ground, dried manure or a bit of driftwood or

whatever, that I could use for the makings of a fire.

I wasn't but a few steps in that direction before it occurred to me that in all the excitement of the evening before I hadn't gotten around to seeing what all my twin had been carrying.

I mean, it wasn't like he'd be needing any of it himself, and it would be a criminal shame to let perfectly good stuff go to waste. If the man had owned any perfectly good stuff, that is.

Seemed only right and proper that I inherit whatever he'd been carrying, us being practically the same as kinfolk in the way we looked so much alike. And besides, hadn't I been right there beside him to offer comfort and solace while he was dying? Of course I had. If he'd died too quick for me to do much in the way of comforting, well, that wasn't my fault but his. I did not hold myself responsible for it.

I went over to where I'd dropped his kak, right there where his horse had been. During the night his horse had buddied up with mine, the way they generally will do, and it was still right there close by even though I hadn't hobbled his gray like I had my own ugly brown critter. I gave them but a glance and looked instead to the saddle and gear that my dead look-alike had owned.

He'd been a traveling man, I surmised, because he carried a pair of oversized saddlebags tied behind his cantle. His bags were a heap finer and more expensive than my own beat-up old things—and whoever said that the owlhoot life is one of riches and good times is, let me tell you, one low-down lying son of a bitch—so instead of just looking into them I untied the saddle strings that held them in place and carried them back closer to the wall of the bluff, where there wasn't quite so much cold wind eddying around and turning my ears to ice.

I mentioned that it was still cold as Satan's breath, didn't I? The dawn made me feel better, but it didn't actually warm things up and the wind was still moaning and grumbling overhead.

I carried the dead guy's stuff back. Had to step over him in the process. He looked even paler and waxier now that he'd been dead awhile, but he didn't seem to be bloating any. See? There are good things can be said for down-deep cold too.

Anyway, I hunkered down by where I wished I had a fire, took a look around the horizon as a matter of habit rather than necessity, then commenced to peek inside and see just what sort of goodies I'd gone and lucked into here.

SEVEN

My oh my. I was rich. That is to say, the dead guy'd been rich. And now by right of inheritance, so was I.

He had . . . took me a while to count it . . . more than $600 in his kick. Or $627 and no stray cents if anyone wants to be precise about it.

That was the second-most amount of money I'd ever held in my hand at one time. The most ever if you wanted to count what part of it was mine. I'd once carried $1,062 out of a bank up in Kansas, but I'd had to share that with two other guys so to my mind it didn't count for near as much as this find did.

And this I hadn't even had to do anything to get hold of except be a good Samaritan to the dead guy.

Add it to the forty-some dollars I was already carrying and I felt downright giddy with all the good luck I was suddenly having.

This dead twin of mine had been more than simply well off financially, I discovered as I went through the rest of his things. He'd also been a man of rare and discriminating good taste . . . He had himself a flask in one pocket of the saddlebags that was near full up with some sort of belly-warming likker. The stuff had a kind of fruity taste to it so maybe it was brandy. Whatever it was, it went down smooth and spread warmth into my belly. I lifted the flask toward the sky in a thank-you toast to the lately deceased and helped myself to a second nip, which was even smoother and lighter on the tongue than the first had been.

Further inspection turned up the usual assortment of dry stuff like flour and rice and ready-ground coffee, none of which is much worth a darn without a fire to cook by, but he'd also been carrying a can of peaches. Which are one of my favorites if a tad on the expensive side for me.

I saw those and right away dragged out my pocketknife. Stabbed a couple holes in the top of the can and drank down the juice first, then sawed the lid open the rest of the way and had a mighty tasty breakfast.

I went back to prowling through the rest of the things in the fellow's saddlebags, but there wasn't all that much of interest. He had the usual assortment of horseshoe nails and one of those pliers-looking multipurpose tools that you can use to shoe a horse or mend a fence wire . . . or cut one if you're mad at a fellow or in a real big hurry. He had a clean shirt, clean underdrawers, clean socks—Lordy, I reckon this had been a tidy fellow so maybe we weren't absolutely identical after all—and a twist of chewing tobacco.

Me, I don't chew. Tried it when I was a kid and didn't like it at all. One of my uncles gave me the chew. I noticed he was the one laughing the loudest when I swallowed some juice and puked my guts out over the back porch railing. I still liked him well enough after that, but I sure knew better than to trust him ever again. And the experience cured me permanent of any desire to chew.

My twin obviously hadn't felt that same way. I put the twist back where I'd found it, thinking I might could use it to swap for something useful, food or whatever, if I met anybody on the trail south.

Rummaging deeper into the dead man's bags, I found a small black folder like tintypes come in, but I didn't mess with it, just shoved it back where I'd found it. I figured that would be a photo of the dead guy's wife, and I didn't want to weigh myself down pitying some poor widow waiting someplace for a man she didn't yet know wouldn't be coming home to her.

I expect I might've been tempted to look if I'd thought it was a picture of some painted up fancygirl. But that kind don't hand out photographic advertisements, and I've never yet seen a picture of anybody's wife that was worth looking at the second time.

Why is it, I've sometimes wondered, that it's the ugly women that marry and breed?

A person would think there ought to be some good-looking wives just because of the sheer numbers of wives out there. But no, every picture you ever see of anybody's wife, she always looks grim as the reaper and laced so tight you could kick her in the belly and your boot would bounce off. Most of them you'd swear couldn't never smile or their face would crack and fall to pieces.

Yet men go out and commit the folly of matrimony on a regular basis.

Maybe there's something to it that I haven't yet figured out.

And, okay, maybe there was something in me that didn't want to draw comparisons between my way of life and whatever this dead look-alike of mine had in his past. Wife, property, family, like that. Maybe that was part of it too. Whatever the reason, I left the leather-bound tintype folder alone and put it back without peeking.

The dead man's saddlebags were a whole lot better than mine, so I transferred my few things into his bigger and nicer bags—well, *my* bigger and nicer ones now—and decided his saddle was the better too.

I kept my old blanket but put his saddle onto my ugly brown thing and strapped all my newfound wealth on behind the cantle. My old saddle went onto the gray horse. Both were worth something, and I figured to sell them and my old and now empty saddlebags next chance I got.

Twin, as I'd taken to calling him in my mind, had had him some wherewithal but he didn't have much judgment when it came to horseflesh. The gray horse he'd been riding was one fine and handsome animal, but it wasn't a patch on the quality of ugly.

To me the quality of a horse hasn't aught to do with what it looks like but in how it performs. My brown is so ugly the dang old thing hurts folks' feelings just to look at it. But the critter is eighty percent heart and the rest all bottom.

It's not a sprinter, and any good cow pony will outrun it. For the first quarter or maybe as much as a half mile.

After that you might as well rein aside because me and old ugly will be kicking gravel in your eyes and leaving nothing but a plume of dust for you to follow.

There just isn't any quit in ugly, and if Twin had been riding him yesterday instead of this handsome gray, the man would've been alive this morning.

So the gear I figured to keep all went onto ugly's back, and the disposable stuff went onto the gray.

I considered what to do with the dead man. I didn't have a shovel. Nor, if the truth be told, much of an inclination to use one.

I settled for checking his pockets . . . came up with another eight dollars in coin there . . . and unbuckling his gun-belt, which was another useful item that could be turned into cash somewhere along the trail.

The fellow hadn't been carrying a long gun, but that was all right as I already had a good one that was now dangling off my new saddle.

He favored a belt knife instead of a pocket model. I dropped that into my old saddlebags as another item to barter or sell.

And that was just about that.

His boots weren't near as nice as the ones I was already wearing, but I did take his spurs to put into the "sell" bag. And naturally checked to see he hadn't been hiding anything inside the boots. He hadn't.

I stood for a minute looking down at him, all pale yellow and shrunken looking, laying there in his sock feet and with his pockets turned inside out.

I didn't know who he was or what he'd been, but for sure this was a poor end for a man to come to.

I stood a moment longer, staring up into the sky. There weren't any buzzards in sight. But that didn't mean anything. They would come along by and by, them and the coyotes and the ants and whatever else might take an interest.

And nobody but me would ever know what it was that happened to this fellow here.

There might be others that would wonder. Like whatever woman it was whose picture was in that folder. But I was the only one that would know.

I scowled a little and decided it was better to avoid dark thoughts or deep ones. Turned away from there and stepped into the saddle on ugly's back.

I wiggled side to side a little and decided this new rig was going to ride just fine, then picked up the lead rope I'd put onto the gray horse and nudged ugly into a walk. We still had us a ways to go to find someplace warm and comfortable.

EIGHT

Brandy in the belly gives off one kind of warmth, but on a cold day there's a better. First chance I found, I got down and made me some coffee.

Four, five miles south of the place where I'd holed up the night before I found a dry wash that had some tangles of dried-up driftwood, splintery pieces of old cedar and the like, collected in pockets along the bottom. And this not being a time of year when I figured I had much to worry about in the way of flash floods—any rain tried to fall in weather like this would end up ice before it could hit the ground, and likely would be blown to Mexico before it could fall anyhow—I worked my way east along the rim until I found a spot where some cattle or something had broke a crossing, then pointed ugly's nose down into the wash.

I came west again to a good spot that had a good-sized heap of wood on the south side, and the northside wall of the wash itself for a windbreak, and figured I was in business. I loosed the cinches on both horses and hobbled ugly, then set about building a fire.

Quick as that was going, and it didn't take long what with the wood already being dry, I took down my canteen and set some water on to boil in the little tin pot that serves me for just about everything that needs doing. Well, everything that has to do with cooking anyhow.

While the water was heating, I made up a batch of dough with some flour and saleratus from the dead guy's stuff and a dab of lard from my own, along with a dribble of warm water out of the pot. There was a greasy twist of paper in with my twin's food that held what looked like real butter, but I didn't want to waste that on stick bread so settled for the lard instead.

By the time the dough was ready, my water was boiling, so I dropped in a palmful of ground coffee, then wrapped my dough around the end of a stick and held it close to the fire, twisting the stick now and then so as to keep the heat even all over. By the time the bread was done, so was the coffee.

Let me tell you, that was one powerful welcome meal, never mind it was a simple one. The coffee was stout and hot and the stick bread warm, and I felt considerable better when I'd finished wrapping myself around them.

I scrubbed out the cooking pot with sand off the floor of the wash, kicked the ashes of my fire apart and pronounced myself fit to live for another day.

I felt so good that even after I climbed back up out of the wash and into the cut of the wind once again, it didn't seem half so cold as it done before.

By midday I was thinking in terms of food again. And was bone-deep cold again. If I'd seen another wash to get down into, I surely would have done it.

Instead I came to a road.

Major sort of road it was too, wide and fairly smooth. Mostly, of course, it was the fact that it was a two-track road that convinced me that it really went somewhere.

Somebody's little old ranch road will nearly always be a narrow three-track because those little shoots and branches generally won't carry but light wagons with a single horse pulling. Freight roads are mostly used by the big rigs with four, six, as much as a dozen animals working in tandem, so those are normally two-track roads but with wider and deeper ruts than the little feeder roads you find running every which way.

Anyway, this one looked to me like there was a good chance it would take me someplace, the next question being was that "place" nearer to the east or to the west.

I stood in my stirrups and gandered off to the east. Then to the west.

With the wind blowing hard from the north, there could've been a forest fire close to either side—well, if there'd been any forests in Texas, that is; I surely had no evidence that such a thing existed in Texas as a forest . . . or even a genuine, full sized tree for that matter—where was I? oh, yes, Forest fire. Wind. Right. Like I was saying, if there'd been a conflagration—how d'you like that word—on either side, I couldn't of seen the smoke for the way that wind would whip it right away.

What I did see, away off to the west and a hair south of the direction the road was aimed, was a tiny touch of purest white, stark against a line of gray cloud low on the horizon in that direction.

Now, unless it's snow or summer cloud, you don't real often see white in nature.

And my belly was rumbling at the notion of someone else's cooking, and my nose and ears could sure benefit from the heat of a potbelly stove.

With those things in mind, I reined ugly west again across the direction of the wind.

I wonder what would've happened if I'd gone east instead.

NINE

What I'd seen from afar off, the white thing spotted low against a gray sky, was the steeple of a church. The church, bright as a new penny, was gleaming in the cold sunshine, and the steeple was the highest thing in view in any direction.

There were some trees scattered about to show there'd been a grove of them to begin with, likely the reason the first guy in the vicinity decided to settle here and start the town to building around him. There were still enough trees to make it impossible for me to see right off how big the town was.

A business district of several wide streets was on the north side, mostly out of the trees. The church sat at the east edge of town, and I could see the roofs and some chimneys of houses in amongst the trees south of the business blocks.

It wasn't a new town. Some of the stores were made of kiln-fired brick, not that cheap homemade adobe stuff like you see some places, and the wood buildings that I could see as I approached were weathered gray.

There wasn't a whole lot of traffic on the streets, but then this was a weekday and most honest folk would be working at their trade, whatever it happened to be. I expected most of the business hereabouts would be the raising of cows. At least that's what I naturally assumed was the major, maybe even the only, business in Texas. How else could the place send so many of the varmints north into Kansas? And so many troublemaking cowboys along with them.

Me and ugly and the dead man's gray clip-clopped slow along the road toward the church and the town beyond it.

I was close enough now to see some people walking to and fro on the boardwalks in front of the stores, and as I came near to the east end of town, I saw a light coach drawn by six small white mules, Spanish mules we'd call them up home, pull away from a place with a two-story false front and head out in my direction.

I moved out of the way to let the coach pass. It wasn't one of those fine and fancy Studebaker heavy rigs, but looked like maybe an old army ambulance that'd been converted for passenger use, so I guessed it was a short-haul outfit that linked this little burg with the big wide world. Gilt lettering on the side of the ambulance declared it represented "The Great Plains and Trans-Mountain Express Co., Inc."

Quite a mouthful, that was, but I didn't take it too serious. I've seen a mountain, and there wasn't one anywhere in prob'ly five hundred miles from whatever town this one was. Nor hardly any decent-sized hills, for that matter.

But then the Texas boys I'd known in the past were sometimes prone to exaggerate. Apparently that trait wasn't limited just to the cowboys down here.

I could see folks walking back and forth, everyone moseying along slow and relaxed. This looked like an easygoing sort of place, and under the circumstances that suited me just fine.

I passed by the church. Didn't pay it all that much attention, if the truth be known, as it had been a right considerable piece of time since I'd last had occasion to step inside one of those.

About the time I was reaching the first of the business buildings, still without seeing any signpost or other indication of what they called their town here, a mound of wool that looked kind of like a dark blue haystack stepped off the end of the last boardwalk and out of the downwind protection of that last building there.

Moving haystack to outward appearance, that is, because the woman was bundled so deep into cape and skirts and bonnet and armloads of packages that I couldn't see any part of a human person under all the covering.

She was dressed for the cold, but I guess she hadn't expected the wind to be blowing as fierce as it was because she'd no sooner lost the protection of the windbreak than her bonnet got plucked right off her head and came sailing south like a kite that's string has broke.

Came right at me since I was unfortunate enough to be caught downwind of this phenomenon. Came hard and fast and on the rise as the wind carried it.

That was all right of itself, I suppose, and I wasn't worried about ugly boogering or getting excited. The dang brown thing is hard to look at, but he's not the least lick spooky. Which is just another of the things I like about him. So I kinda sat where I was and marveled at the speed of that wind-carried bonnet.

What I should have been doing was getting out of the way. Because what I'd forgot was that ugly wouldn't booger or scare, but me and ugly weren't entirely alone here. And the dead man's fine-looking gray critter hadn't ugly's good sense when it came to standing fast.

The gray threw its head and rolled its eyes and tried to run away.

Tried to bolt straight up ugly's backside, actually.

To which ugly took serious exception.

Next thing I knew the two of them were in a storm, ears pinned and hoofs thumping and me setting in the middle of the fight.

Ugly kicked the gray a couple good licks on the forequarters, and the gray tried to take a bite out of ugly, missed and bit the side of my boot instead.

I tried to kick the gray in the muzzle but missed because without warning I couldn't see anything due to the fact that the flying bonnet that'd started this mess hit me in the face. The wind drove it up under my chin, and some flapping pieces of cloth—if the stupid woman had tied those things to begin with, none of this would've happened—flew up in my eyes.

For about a minute and a half there the three of us stayed almighty busy, until I could get both horses to keep all four hoofs on the ground and clawed that dumb lady's hat off my face.

I finally got everything and everybody to settle down and then, pretty well peeved by that time, reined ugly to the right, toward the stupid woman who'd caused the problem.

What I intended was to give this female person a piece of my mind about scaring folks' mounts and common consideration for others and such-like as all that.

What I did instead was sit there blinking and staring down from atop my ugly old brown horse.

I was sitting there looking down at the purantee prettiest female creature that has ever drawn breath.

TEN

I'm sure I was rude, staring at her like that. But I couldn't help it. This girl was . . . I don't rightly know how to put it. I mean, it isn't like I've never been around girls before. I have. Lots of them. A couple of those were decent girls, even. But this one, well, she was special.

She had the biggest, widest, clearest eyes I've ever seen. Pale, they were, gray and sorta green and flecked with bits of gold. I don't know what you call that, but they were pretty, I can sure say that much.

She had freckles, and right then her cheeks were red and glowing. Now, I know that had to do with the cold and the wind. Of course it did.

Her nose was thin and nipped off short and square at the tip end, and her lips . . . well, that didn't bear thinking on. Her lips looked so soft and sweet that it was all I could do to stay up on top of old ugly where I belonged.

Her hair, whipping in the breeze and all a-tangle now she hadn't a bonnet on, was a light, coppery red. Not *red* red. Exactly. But for sure not yellow either. I couldn't tell how she normally wore it but suspected that this mouse-nest do wasn't her usual style.

She had round cheeks and a pert little chin and dimples, actual dimples.

As for the rest of her, well, I couldn't tell about that,

what with her being bundled inside more wrappings than a cart could carry. She might've been shaped like a turnip for all I could tell by looking at that particular moment. But d'you want to know something really odd? I don't think I would've cared if she was built like a bass fiddle. She was so cute and dandy looking that I don't think I would've minded it the least little bit.

Not that I expected ever to find out, of course. I was just passing through whatever place this was and had no intention of stopping, not even to sidle up beside a girl this pretty. Now if she'd been some painted dove, and me with money in my pockets for a change, I expect I might've hung around a spell for that. But it didn't take any extra special powers of observation to tell that this girl was decency and class clear through to the bone. One look into those eyes was enough to make that plain.

And oh, I was enjoying looking down into those pretty eyes of hers. Kept on doing it on and on and then some.

Slow and gradual-like her expression changed from the casual smile she'd started out with, melted into one of mild annoyance and then toward what might've been taken for a hint of concern.

"Sir? Is something wrong, sir?" She sounded genuinely puzzled, and it took me a moment to figure out why.

Then I realized that all this time she'd been standing at my right stirrup with her hand held out and an expectant sort of look on her.

And it finally got through to me that I wasn't only staring hard at her, I was clinging to her wrinkled and mussed-up bonnet at the same time.

Cold as the wind was, I felt some heat come into my cheeks just then.

Feeling sheepish and ignorant, I draped my reins over ugly's scrawny neck and tried to straighten out her crumpled bonnet, realized I wasn't doing it any good by the attempt and settled for just handing the thing back to her.

"Thank you," she said, and the smile returned. Lordy, I would've done handstands and cartwheels right there in the middle of the street if I'd thought it would make that girl smile again.

I pondered asking her name and where she lived. But I never.

This was an honest girl, a good girl, I could tell that. A girl like that wouldn't have use for a fella with my particular background.

Now, don't get me wrong about that. I've found in the past that word going around that a man is on the dodge with posters advertising a price on his head, well, that can be a real strong attraction to some women. Even some that you'd have swore was upright and tied tight in their laces. Choir singers, married ladies—it's purely amazing the way some women will act when they get the idea there's something dangerous and exciting about a man.

I don't know what the attraction is. But the truth is that I've never been known to voice objections when a situation like that came up.

This girl, though . . . she wasn't like that. I could see it plain as daylight. This one was a lady. The real thing.

I shoved the bonnet back at her and bobbed my head and touched the brim of my beat-up old hat to her. And hoped the fire in my cheeks didn't show or that at the very least she'd take it to be the cold wind causing any red in my face.

"Ma'am." I remembered now that I'd had it in mind to tell the lady off for letting her bonnet get away and spook my animals.

That didn't seem so gosh-awful important to me now, and I let the chance pass by untaken.

"Thank you, sir."

"Yes'm. Any time." I meant that most sincerely too. Any time at all. I'd sure come running.

I touched my hat brim again and the girl—I sure wished I knew her name—gave me a look that seemed . . . No, I expect not. Not really. I guess wishful thinking was playing tricks on my imagination.

The girl backed half a pace away, still looking at me, and I nudged old ugly into a slow walk, turning half around in my saddle so as to keep that pretty face in view a few seconds longer.

She stood right where she was for half a dozen heartbeats, then crumpled the bonnet in her hand—she prob'ly couldn't put it on since she was still juggling a heap of small packages in her other arm—and started running downwind across the street behind me.

She skipped up the stone steps of the church building I'd just passed and disappeared inside it.

After that I nudged ugly again—he'd quit walking, though I didn't recall ever telling him to—and headed the rest of the way on into the town.

ELEVEN

Never did a cup of coffee taste so good. The sign out front said "Cafe," and the smells inside confirmed it. This right here was the place I'd been looking for all the day long.

The waiter was a cheerful enough sort with an apron that wasn't too awful dirty and hands that looked clean. And he'd brought me the cup of coffee, aromatic steam lifting off the dark surface of it, without having to be asked. That too was a good indication, so I didn't even bother inspecting the chalkboard to see what was available. I figured the day's special here would be good and told the man so.

The special turned out to be prob'ly the best beef stew I've laid a tongue to since I last had my mama's cooking. I got around the first bowl in record time and kept myself busy with a basket of yeast rolls while I motioned for a refill. Time I was done stuffing myself with stew and buttered rolls, I practically didn't have room for the dried apple pie that came after. I had to settle for just one slice, and that seemed a shame.

"Hungry," the waiter observed when I went to pay up. I grinned at him. "Not now, I'm not."

"I'll have to charge you extra for the second bowl."

"That's fair enough. And I'd've had a third if I could've held it."

"Regular is fifteen cents for the lunch. Twenty cents be all right with you instead?"

I gave him a quarter and didn't ask for no change back, I was that pleased.

I took a look outside the window and thought about the cut of that wind out there blowing dust and leaves, and for all I knew flinging pea gravel around the countryside too . . . then thought about the promise of having supper too in a place with food this good. Maybe I wasn't in such a hurry to get south as I'd thought I was. I turned back to the waiter.

"Anyplace in town where a man can find a clean room for himself and a bait of grain for his horses?"

The fellow gave me directions, first to a livery at the west end of town, then to a hotel two blocks back this direction and a block south of the main street.

"The place doesn't look like much," the waiter said, "but you'll like it."

"Sure enough?"

He smiled. "It's either that or spread your blankets outdoors someplace. Old Alex down at the livery barn won't let anybody sleep inside like you'd expect. He's scared somebody will start a fire."

"I don't smoke," I told the man.

"You know, that's the same thing the last fellow told Alex when he asked could he stay overnight."

"Yes?"

"Made Alex real mad when the fellow up and burned the barn down anyhow. Said he was trying to light a lantern. Alex, he isn't so trusting now as he used to be."

"Uh huh," I said. "Reckon I'll try the hotel."

"You do that, friend. Tell them Johnny sent you."

"Will that get me a better rate?"

The waiter laughed. "Probably not, but the same fellow that owns the hotel owns one of the saloons in town too, so it will get me a free drink next time I stop in."

"I'll be sure and tell them that Johnny sent me." I went back outside, feeling better now than I'd felt in days, warmer and fuller and in generally high spirits.

TWELVE

I guess the one fellow did own both the hotel and saloon for the two of them was connected so close there was even a door cut into the wall of the hotel lobby so a person could go from the one into the other and never have to step out into the cold. Convenient is what I'd call that, downright convenient.

Just to sort of check on that comfort theory, I came back downstairs—the hotel was two stories high—soon as I'd put my stuff in the room and walked through that connecting door. And sure enough, I was just as comfortable as could be whilst walking from the hotel to the watering hole.

There was an iron stove purring over in the hotel side and another in the saloon, and all in all a fella could stay toasty warm with this kind of arrangement.

It was still early in the afternoon so there weren't a whole lot of drinkers lined up in the saloon, just a couple men at the bar nursing mugs of beer that they must've been working on for some considerable time. Either that or the saloon served its beer flat to begin with. There were those two, both of them dressed shabby, like down-on-their-luck cowhands who would've been out riding the grub line if it wasn't so dang cold and windy outside, and off in a back corner there were three gents who had a somewhat more prosperous look about them, these ones dressed for town type business. The three city types were at a table, huddled around a bottle and glasses.

The barman looked friendly enough. Fat. I always like a fat man. I know I can outrun him if ever I have to.

Not that I expected to be getting into any mischief here in . . . It occurred to me that I still hadn't seen nor heard the name of this place, whatever it was . . . Anyhow, I wasn't expecting no trouble here. No reason for it. After all, I had cash money in my pocket and a fine meal behind my belt. And there wasn't any reason to call attention to myself now that I was down here where the printed notices might not tag along behind me. I was clean and clear in Texas and wanted to keep it that way. Figured I would just lay over here relaxing and taking things easy for the next few days, until this cold and wind slacked off, then me and my dead twin's money would be on our way again.

With luck maybe I could find me a buyer for the gray horse and other stuff that I didn't need and actually ride away with my pockets heavier than they already were.

I ambled over to the bar and gave the fat man a nod and a smile. The barman, he glanced to the left and the right, like as if he was checking to see if anybody was close enough to overhear, before he asked me what I wanted. Well, folks sometimes are a mite peculiar. If I started holding that against everybody that ever did anything odd I expect I'd end up with a grudge toward just about everyone I ever knew. I ignored it and asked for a beer. If I'd intended going outside again I would've been more interested in whiskey to keep the fires stoked in my belly, but beer is what I generally like, especially when I'm feeling warm and easy.

The fat man brought my beer. With a full head on it, proving that the loafers down to my left had more time on their hands than they had money to fill it.

I've been broke my own self more than a few times, and I know how it is. On an impulse I motioned the barman back over after I'd taken that first bitter-bright swallow and said, "Draw fresh ones for those boys down the way. On me."

The barman nodded and took up a pair of mugs. I looked the other way, back toward the businessmen in their corner, so it wouldn't seem I was watching the cowboys and hankering for a lot of hoohah and thank-yous.

I heard a little mumbling and then a slightly louder "thanks, mister" that I ignored, and the fat man walked past me and out from behind his bar. He carried a bowl of peanuts to the table in the back although there was already a near full bowl sitting there along with the bottle and glasses.

The barman leaned down and whispered something to one of the three men, then came back behind the bar and took to washing glassware that already looked clean.

Me, I had another swallow of my beer. It went down even nicer than the first had, so I finished that beer and waved for another.

I was, I figured, settled in for the rest of the day.

THIRTEEN

The cowboys eventually got tired of sipping slow at warm beer, bundled themselves into coats and slickers and dragged their hats low over their eyes before braving the outdoors. When they went out, they let a blast of frigid air in that reminded me how much better it was in here than out there. I celebrated the thought with another beer.

The fat man brought it, collected the price out of the change lying on the bar in front of me and glanced once past my shoulder before making himself busy at the far end of the bar.

A moment later I realized why he'd taken himself so far away. One of the gents from the table in back sidled up beside me and looked around slow and careful before speaking in a voice that was scarcely above a whisper.

"I want you to know, Marshall, that we're ready to help out any way we can."

I guess I blinked a couple times before I got wits enough about me to make an answer to that. "That's fine, friend, but who might you be?"

He leaned a mite closer, dropped his voice even lower so that even though he was practically breathing into my ear now, I could barely hear. For sure nobody else could've.

"Name's Tolliver. George Tolliver. I'm the mayor. All right?"

"Please t'meet you I'm sure, Mayor Tolliver, but I expect you've got me mixed up with somebody else." I could guess who easy enough, but of course I didn't exactly come right out and say that.

The mayor leaned closer yet, and this time I could for sure feel the heat of his breath on my ear. "It's all right, Marshall. Amos there," he inclined his head in the direction of the fat man down at the far end of the bar, "Amos recognized you right off when you came in. Saw you in Austin one time, he says. In Judge Wickstrom's courtroom?" I don't know that Tolliver intended that to be a question, but he kinda made it sound like it was. Was or wasn't, though, I wasn't answering it. I mean . . . who the hell was this judge fella anyway? And what would my twin have been taken in front of him for? Lordy, I hoped the *both* of us weren't wanted. It would of been just too goldarn much for me to come south of the Wants out for me only to step into a look-alike's troubles instead. If there was paper out on my dead twin, it was something I should ought to know. I realized that right there on the spot.

But I still couldn't hardly go and say much of anything, seeing as how I hadn't the least idea what this man was talking about.

Turned out the honorable mayor didn't need any answers from me. Seemed he was supplying them for himself. Making assumptions and like that.

"We won't give you away, Marshall," he whispered real low. "We've already told Amos not to tell anyone else who you are, and we'll stand behind you all the way."

I grunted a little, figuring he could take that to mean anything he wanted. And he did.

"Remember what I said. Anything you need, you come to me or one of the town fathers over there at that table. The gentleman on the left is our county sheriff, Herb Frake. The man on the right is Carlton Brainard. Carlton is the banker. You can trust any of the three of us. We won't let it out who you really are."

"Good," I said, breathing somewhat easier. I didn't have to make up any part of that as it was surely as true as anything ever could be. Good enough and better than that.

The mayor, the banker and the sheriff were all behind me. Now that was surely nice to know. It meant that this Marshall fellow ... whoever and whatever he was ... couldn't be wanted for anything down here. He had a pretty clean bill of health if gents like those three were backing him.

And the more I thought about it, the nicer this deal was commencing to sound.

I mean, a banker wanted to help me out?

I hadn't known there was a bank in this dinky town. Now I not only discovered there was a bank, I knew that the banker was on my side.

My side of ... whatever.

Sounded pretty good, though.

Maybe me and my twin could make a withdrawal.

It was an idea that kinda appealed to me. I'd made a fair good many bank withdrawals in my time, you see. But I'd never made one that I didn't have a gun in my hand at the time.

The novelty of doing it some other way seemed sorta fetching.

Of course there were a couple things I was gonna have to figure out first. Like was Marshall my first name or last? And just what was it that these fine folk expected to help me with? And how far could that assistance be pushed to convert good intentions into hard currency?

My oh my, I did have me some thinking to do.

The front door to the saloon pushed open, sweeping in another blast of cold ahead of a couple hard-looking cowboys, different ones this time, and His Honor the mayor gave them a quick glance and then kinda melted away from beside me and went back to the table he was sharing with Mr. Brainard and Sheriff Frake.

Nossir, butter wouldn't have melted in the mayor's mouth, nor could anybody've figured out that him and me had just been whispering back and forth.

I wasn't for sure yet what I ought to do here, but I didn't

want to burn no bridges until I had a better handle on this thing, so I gave the three gents in back a wink that the cowboys couldn't see, then turned and ambled on out of there and up to my room. I figured I could use me some privacy and a little deep thinking before I did anything else.

FOURTEEN

The hotel room wasn't much, just a cot with a hard canvas surface to sleep on, a table with a lamp on it, a stool to sit on and some pegs driven into the wall to serve as a wardrobe. But then just like the man at the cafe told me, it was a whole heap better than spreading my blankets outdoors.

I kicked my boots off and stretched out with the skimpy little bit of a thing that was passed off here for a pillow wadded up and stuffed between the wall and the back of my neck.

There wasn't any stove in the room, but a floor register let in warm air from downstairs so it was pretty comfortable. I could hear the wind rattling the window, and that was more than enough of a reminder of how good I was having it if I found myself needing one.

I lay there for a while trying to figure out how to turn this strange deal to best advantage.

Whoever Marshall had been—and I pretty much had to conclude that the dead guy was him—it sure would've been a help to me if he'd carried something on him to show it.

The mayor'd said they wouldn't none of them tell on me—well, him really—about who I was or why I was here. So the mayor and his friends knew something about Marshal. Or anyway thought they did. And they were willing to help.

That covered a mighty wide range of possibilities, and it would've helped me considerable if I could get some sort of handle on what they knew, or thought they knew, so I could make a plan to fit.

I suppose it would be too much to ask for Marshall to've had a bank account of his own here.

Although I couldn't help but grin and chuckle at the thought of it.

It would've been a marvel to just walk into a bank and sign a slip of paper and walk out with . . . what the heck, if you're going to dream anyway you might as well dream big . . . let's say walk out with a couple thousand dollars in hand.

Which didn't seem all that unreasonable when I thought about it some more. After all, any man who walks around carrying six hundred might could have six thousand tucked away in a bank somewhere.

Lordy, if I could only find out some more about Marshall. His full name. Where he came from. Where he banked. All that stuff. Sure would be something to find his bank and go clean it out. And nobody shooting at me on my way out the door.

I'd need a look at his signature so I could copy it. And . . . aw, there wasn't any sense in getting worked up about it.

The plain fact was that Marshall hadn't been carrying any letters or bankbooks or anything so convenient as to tell me all I wanted to know now.

Probably my best hope here was to just let things lay and enjoy the good fortune I'd had so far. Maybe get the mayor and the banker and them to buy the gray horse and other spare stuff off me and then ride south again once the storm blew itself out.

On the other hand, well, a fellow can't hardly be blamed for *thinking* about things.

So I lay there warm and comfortable, my belly full and nobody after my scalp, and while I thought about Marshall and how to make some use of the way the two of us had looked so much alike, I sort of lost the rest of that afternoon and may even have snored just a little. Although that, I hasten to say, is only rumor spread by other folks as I personally have never heard me snore and therefore am suspicious as to the true cause of their complaining.

FIFTEEN

The hotel didn't have a restaurant attached to it, so if I wanted to eat there it would have to be off the free lunch spread in the saloon next door.

Now, there's been many and many a time that I've eat my fill of free lunches. But never when I had money in my pockets to pay for something worth putting into a man's stomach.

Free lunches always run to the same tired old stuff. Slices of ham so dried out they look, feel and taste more like jerky than ham. Pickled eggs so sour they make my belly churn just from thinking about them. Salty peanuts to make you thirsty. And dry, crumbling hunks of cheese with fly specks all over them.

No, given any choice at all, free lunches just aren't generally worth what you have to pay for them.

Come suppertime, I yawned a mite and rubbed the sleep out of my eyes and bundled myself deep inside my coat. It occurred to me that I could afford to buy some gloves now instead of having to rely on old socks pulled over my hands.

But then again, if I was going to keep on riding south, buying gloves would just be a waste, wouldn't it?

For the time being I settled for leaving the socks in my room and shoving my hands into my coat pockets for the walk to the cafe where I'd had lunch earlier.

It was cold enough in that wind to shrivel your dauber, but the cafe wasn't so awful far away and I was starting out warm to begin with, so I got there without anything important freezing and falling off, and quick as I got inside, opened my coat to let the warmth reach me. I hung my coat and hat on a rack beside the door and took a seat at a table close to the stove as there wasn't much in the way of trade being done. I didn't know if the hour was wrong or if they just didn't do much evening business here, but there was plenty of room in the place.

Johnny, the waiter from lunch, was working suppers too. He must of remembered me, for he smiled and nodded a hello, then brought a cup of coffee without having to be asked.

"The special again tonight?"

"Same stew as before?"

"It is."

"You wouldn't be able to find me a steak, would you? Something about this-here thick, fried so it's done clear through, maybe some gravy piled on top?"

"I could do that."

"And some potatoes. Fry them too and keep the gravy coming."

"Fifty cents for all that," Johnny warned.

"I'm good for it."

"It won't be but a little while. You want your pie for while you're waiting?"

"You bet."

The pie was even better than I remembered it being, and the steak that followed was as good as I've had in a long while. I packed myself till I like to burst, then sopped up what gravy was left with a few final biscuits. By then I wasn't real sure I could make it back to the hotel unassisted, but might have to get Johnny to call for a couple strong men to carry me outside and load me into a wagon.

The thought of going back out into that wind wasn't particularly inviting, but as far as I could tell they didn't rent bed space at the cafe, so eventually I forced myself to stand up despite the weight of all that good food laying warm in my belly.

I left a half-dollar piece and a silver half-dime on the table, fetched down my coat and hat, buttoned up tight and waved to Johnny on the way out.

I wasn't halfway back to the hotel when some idjit, a drunk more than likely, went to spraying the street with bullets.

SIXTEEN

Now, it is one thing to have fun making noise. Heck, I've done that my own self on New Year's, Fourth of July, times like that. I suppose I've even done it now and then without any more of an excuse than that I'd been taken drunk.

But danggit, guns aren't just loud, they're also dangerous. And this fool wasn't shooting into the air like a body will for the tomfoolery of it, he was shooting flat along the ground, shooting more or less down the length of the town street.

That wouldn't have been so awful bad except that I happened to be walking in that street at the time, and some of those bullets were hitting close enough to sting my pant legs with gravel.

That was bad enough. What was worse was that you just never know where a ricochet will fly. Anything that can pepper you with gravel can just as easy hit you with solid lead if the ricochet takes it the wrong way.

Now, I don't claim to be smart, but it don't take me real long to let go of a pot handle that's hot out of an oven . . . or to get out of the way when some drunk is shooting bullets my way.

I jumped right quick into the mouth of an alley and

pressed my back tight to the wall of whatever store it was that was sheltering me.

The drunk must of seen it when I moved and maybe realized what he'd done, for he stopped shooting then. I heard a shout off in the direction the bullets had come from and then heard footsteps loud on the frozen ground of the street. It sounded like a couple fellows were running. Huh. They were lucky they still had balance enough to run without falling down and busting their own noses, for a fellow surely had to be pretty darn drunk to cut loose with firearms down a public street like they'd done.

I didn't want to risk running into either of them again, so I stayed right where I was—at least the angle of it was such that the wind wasn't funneling through the alley or I couldn't of stood being there for more than a minute or so—until I was pretty sure those boys'd had time enough to get far away and then some.

After that, let me tell you, I held close to the fronts of the buildings I passed and kept an eye out for holes to bolt into should the shooting crank up for another round.

Fortunately I didn't see nor hear any more from the playful shooters and made it safely back to the hotel, where the heat coming out of that potbelly stove was more than merely welcome.

I nodded to the night clerk and gave about half a second's thought to stepping into the saloon for a drink to kind of settle things in my stomach, then thought better of that.

I'd had about enough of drunks for one night, thank you, and didn't want to risk running into any others. Figured even if the next party was innocent, I just might be tempted to blow off steam by rearranging his face for him. I'm not particularly proud of it, but that is something that I've been known to do from time to time.

Instead of that, I settled for going upstairs and going to bed.

SEVENTEEN

I woke to silence. That seemed so ordinary and natural that at first I didn't think anything of it, just kind of rolled around and rooted my ears a little deeper into the flat, scrawny bit of a thing they were trying to pass off as a pillow.

Then I realized what it was about the silence that sounded so loud.

It'd been days now since I'd heard actual quiet. I mean, it had been days and days now that underneath any and every other sound there was always the sound of a brittle wind keening by.

The cold wind was gone now, and that meant I could think about heading south again just as quick as I could get some breakfast behind my belt buckle and saddle my horse. Horses. Whatever.

Once I realized that, I was wide, wide awake. I got up and clomped barefoot across the icy floorboards to peer out the window.

And found nothing out there but solid white.

Not fog white neither. Snow white. The wind was gone and apparently so was the cold or anyway the down deep worst of the cold, but what replaced it wasn't all that much better, for now it was snowing just as hard as before it'd been blowing.

I couldn't see enough to tell how much snow had already fallen, but then I didn't particularly need to know that. Just one look outside the window and I could see that it was too much for comfort, and it was still coming down thick and heavy.

The thing is, in flat country like it was hereabouts, snow can do strange things. It will fall and you not think much about it. Next thing you know a wind kicks up, and that snow begins to rearrange itself. While the wind is blowing and the snow is moving, it's like a thick white blanket has been laid over everything. You can't see nor hear nor hardly figure out which direction is what.

That's bad enough, but isn't the half of the problem, because then the miserable stuff collects in low spots, forms drifts and cornices, does Lord only knows what sort of nastiness.

Man or horse either one can get caught inside a drift, at the bottom of a gully, say, where you might think it would be safe to shelter out of the wind, and be buried ten feet under. Folks can end up dead that way. I know. Up home once I was caught afoot—an unlucky shot by a shotgun messenger pinked my horse and bled him to death slow, but fortunately for me nobody behind me knew that or suspected that I'd be unhorsed and easy prey did they want to chase after me—caught afoot, like I was saying, and tumbled into a ditch that'd drifted full.

I wasn't six feet from bare, solid ground, but it might could have been six miles instead. The snow was the wet, heavy kind, and it wouldn't leave be. The more I struggled and squirmed, the deeper into it I sank. Before too awful long I wasn't just wet through to the skin and getting colder every second, I was purely wore out from wallowing about chest-deep in the drift.

I thought I was a goner then. I truly did. And I still think on that as prob'ly the closest I've yet come to dying.

The only thing that saved me was that I wore out so completely that I couldn't fight it anymore. I gave up. For that little while there I did. I gave up. I kinda slumped back and closed my eyes and expected to lay there and die of freezing or exhaustion or . . . I dunno what else.

Then after a spell, when I'd rested some, I got mad instead. And I would have to admit that I've got something of a temper at times.

Well, this time I got mad. But I was still scared enough to settle back and do some thinking instead of just trying to bull my way out of the drift, which hadn't done me very much good up to that point and didn't seem likely to get any better if I went back to it.

What I finally figured out was that I was gonna have to treat that snow like it was water and sort of float or swim across the top of it. The tricky part was getting myself up more or less horizontal in and on the snow where my flailing had packed it. Then it wasn't so much to roll and bellycrawl those lousy couple of feet to the side of the ditch where I could get ahold of some solid earth.

I got out of that one, but I've been more than half-scared of snowdrifts ever since and wasn't about to set out south again until I could be sure ugly and me wouldn't be walking into any drift-filled gullies or like that.

Which meant there wasn't any reason at all to be hurrying down to the livery stable to grab my horses and get.

I thought about breakfast. Thought about walking through the snow to get to the cafe. Then went back to bed and pulled the blanket up over my head. There'd be time enough for breakfast later. Like maybe at lunchtime.

EIGHTEEN

I took another look out the window and decided that dried-out ham and pickled eggs sounded pretty good for breakfast. Better than going outside, anyhow.

I had no idea what time it was. I've never owned a watch, and with the sky full of falling snow, I couldn't check to see where the sun was. Daytime. That was close enough. I yawned a little, stretched lazy muscles, pulled on some clothes and went downstairs.

Probably because of the weather, the saloon was doing a good business. There were three cowboys down at one end of the bar. I thought I'd seen at least two of them yesterday, but wasn't for sure about that. A couple of men wearing fur hats and rubber overshoes were playing cards at a table, and in the same back corner as before, the mayor and his cronies, including a gent I hadn't seen earlier, were bent over bowls of something hot enough to steam.

Hot sounded pretty good to me, better than pickled eggs, so I motioned the fat bartender Amos closer and pointed. "I'd like some of whatever they're having."

"Sure thing. You want a beer with that?"

"You got coffee?"

"Nope. Got beer or whiskey. You want anything else, you got to go someplace else."

"Whiskey," I said.

"And stew."

"That's right."

Amos grunted, poured my whiskey first and then disappeared into the back of the place somewhere in search of the stew.

The whiskey wasn't bad. But then a lot of places do that. The first knock or two are the good stuff. Then about the time your tongue is getting numb, they switch to the bottle of cheap goods. I know that but don't particularly mind it. After all, by then it all tastes the same anyhow, so why should I care?

Amos came back with my stew. It was hot, I'll give it that much. The steam was lifting off the brown, greasy surface. There were some lumps hiding inside the gravy. I wasn't sure what those were. I tasted of a couple of them. Still wasn't sure.

Down at the far end of the bar, the cowboys kept giving me sidelong glances, and I had to wonder if maybe one or two of those boys had been feeling playful last evening. They were all wearing guns. I considered bringing the subject up but decided against it. Like I said. There were three of them. And they were all wearing guns. I had some more of the stew and wondered if I should've gone for the pickled eggs instead. At least I knew what those were and where they came from. Although come to think of it, when you give some thought to just where it is that an egg does come from . . .

The banker Brainard got up from the table where the mayor and friends were eating. He came over to the bar and started piling some cheese and hard crackers onto a plate to carry back.

I felt a light tap on my shoulder and turned to see the clerk that'd been in the hotel lobby when I came downstairs.

"Sir."

"Mmm?"

"You didn't sign the register when you checked in."

"Didn't I?" I knew that I didn't, of course. It's a habit. I don't always want to let folks know who or where I am. Just in case somebody unfriendly becomes interested.

"No, sir. And, uh, perhaps you would give me your name, sir."

I noticed that he didn't ask me to come back out and sign the book. Very thoughtful of him. It so happens that I can read and cipher just fine, but a lot can't. This boy didn't want to embarrass me if an X would've been all I could provide on my own.

"Sure, son. It's Marshall."

He stood there, waiting for the rest of it, although I'd hoped he would let it go at the one name, seeing as I didn't know whether Marshall was supposed to be my first name or last.

"Yes, sir?"

"George," I told him. "George Marshall." It was the first name that popped into my mind, being the town mayor's name also.

"Very good, sir. I'll note that in the guest register. Thanks for your time, sir."

I nodded to the boy and turned back around.

Brainard was still there, still piling slivers of cheese onto a plate that was already overloaded with the stuff. The banker looked kinda amused. He shot a furtive glance past me toward the cowboys, then as he turned to head back to his table, he whispered, "Now *that* was funny."

If he said so—though I didn't quite see how. Me, I didn't say anything back at him but pretended like I hadn't heard.

Brainard carried his peck of cheese back to join the other fellows, and I went back to trying to figure out what was in this stuff that I was eating.

NINETEEN

Come suppertime, I surely did not want to repeat my lunch-for-breakfast experience. I still had a slightly queasy stomach from the aftereffects of that stew, and the thought of the junk on the free lunch spread was almost as bad.

It was snowing out, although still without wind today. I considered it and decided the walk to the cafe would be worth the trouble involved, so I went upstairs and got my coat.

The boy at the desk smiled nice and pleasant when I came back down. I nodded a howdy to him and headed for the street.

It wasn't near as cold outside as it had been the past few days. I tugged my hat down tight and stuffed my hands deep into my pockets and headed off down the sidewalk.

One nice thing about staying indoors most of the day was that by now the sidewalks had been shoveled clear. There was snow continuing to fall, but most of it had already been pushed off into the street, so as long as I held close to the fronts of the buildings, I wouldn't have to wade through any deep stuff except for when I crossed from one block of buildings to the next. I appreciated that.

I walked up to the main street and turned toward the cafe. Thought for maybe a second about going the other way, out to the livery to check on how ugly and the gray horse were being tended. But heck, the man that ran the stable—I couldn't call his name to mind right at the time—he'd seemed a reliable sort. I was sure I could trust him to do right by the stock under his care.

And besides, there was a gap in the business buildings down that way where I figured no one would have been out shoveling and sweeping. I wasn't much in the mood to be shoving my way through knee-deep snow, so kept on toward the cafe instead.

I still wasn't for sure just what the time of day might be. It was near dark, but of course the solid, snow-heavy overcast played a part in that. Somewhere along toward the late afternoon, I guessed. Late enough, anyway, for me to be hungry again.

I passed a mercantile and thought about stepping inside to buy some gloves. Soft ones, maybe, with rabbit-fur lining. Those are warm, and warm would be nice if the weather down here in supposedly winter-hot Texas was going to keep on being just the same as I'd always found it up north.

Thought about it and had the money in my pockets to pay for whatever I wanted in there, but I passed on by anyhow.

There was a lamp burning on the counter. I could see that as I walked by. But I couldn't see any customers inside, nor any sign of the proprietor. On a day like this I wouldn't have blamed him for locking up early and going home to see what Mama had in the oven.

Anyway, I thought about buying gloves but never actually got around to trying the door to see if it was open or not.

The cafe was just in the next block east, and I could already as good as taste the biscuits Johnny served there and the dried apple pie to go with them.

Pie before supper had gone down just fine last night, and I was thinking about doing the same again tonight. My mouth was already watering at the thought, and I think I stepped out a little livelier at the memory of how that pie tasted.

I hadn't any more than done that than I felt a thump high in my back, somewhere to the right of center, that felt like a mule had sneaked up behind and kicked me there with both feet.

I felt the shock of being struck there and next thing I knew had my face buried in snow, my mouth and nose and eyes all packed cold and wet with it.

I was facedown in the street but had no idea how I'd gotten that way. I knew, sort of, that I'd taken a fall, but I had no memory of doing it.

I did, however, know right away what it was that happened.

Had no doubt about that.

But then, you see, I've been shot before.

TWENTY

There was good news and there was bad news. I was alive. And that was the news. In both categories.

Lordy, but I did hurt. I felt like my chest was clamped into a blacksmith's vise. Hard. And then, dang it, set on fire too.

Breathing was just about more pain than I wanted to go through. I couldn't stop it altogether, but I sure tried to do it as little as possible.

I couldn't see anything, couldn't hear anything, could only feel. Wished I couldn't do that either.

I was . . . warm, that's what I was. The last thing I remembered I'd been facedown in a blanket of snow. Now I was warm enough and dry too.

Wasn't dead, though. That surely would have stopped the hurting. I gave the possibility real serious consideration and might've just tipped the scales in that direction—it hurt that awful bad—except the choice wasn't mine to make. I just kept on laying there, hurting, enduring one hateful breath after another, until after a while the sense of feeling sort of slipped and slid out of reach, and I guess I went back under to wherever I'd been lately.

I could feel again—still couldn't see or hear, but by golly I could sure smell something. It smelled warm and nice and comforting, and I knew it was something that I'd smelled before, although I couldn't recall what it might be or how I'd come to know of it.

Then I remembered, and I wondered if maybe I'd died after all and this was a kind of looking back to when I was a tadpole, because what I would've swore I was smelling was chicken soup.

My mother had always believed that chicken soup was a sovereign remedy for anything that ailed one, and when I was little I could count on having chicken soup anytime I got a hurt or a sniffle.

I hadn't had chicken soup in . . . well, ever since that time, I guessed . . . and now here I was laying shot in the back in some Texas town that I didn't even know the name of, and I was smelling chicken soup. No, I wasn't at all sure that I hadn't gone and died a while back there when I wasn't paying attention.

Chicken soup. The smell of it was so strong it made my mouth water. Lordy, but that did smell good.

Made my stomach rumble just from smelling of it.

And that right there convinced me that I was pretty surely still alive, like it or not.

If I could just get a wee small taste of the chicken soup, why, maybe I'd not be unhappy about the prospects of survival after all.

Which led to another small realization, and that was that the hurting wasn't near so bad as it had been.

Oh, it was bad. Breathing remained an exercise in agony. But the cutting edge of the pain wasn't quite so sharp now as it had been. It was like the knives that were stabbing into my chest had been dulled just the least little bit, and the stabbing was not quite so constant nor quite so deep.

As improvements go, this one wasn't much, but it sure beat taking things in the other direction. I was willing to settle for what I had. If I could just have some of that soup, that is.

I heard something then. A soft, scraping sound like something rubbing over wood. Then a very faint rustling noise.

And after that I could see, sort of. There was the sound

like cloth moving against cloth and then a brightness off to my right.

I heard more of the wood sounds and recognized them then as light footsteps. They moved from my right, over by where the light was, across to my left. And then closer. And the closer the footsteps came the better I could smell the chicken soup.

It got so I figured I was either going to have to have me some of that soup or drown in my own saliva.

Of a sudden I got so hungry there were cramps in my belly, and for half a second there I almost forgot the pain in my chest.

Then without warning the light and the sound and the smells all went away again.

TWENTY-ONE

Next time I woke up, things weren't quite so fuzzy. I was still miserable, you understand. I hurt so bad I liked to cried. But at least I knew that there was an actual world out there around me.

Of course it was something of a mystery to me just what part of that world I was in. I mean, I'd never seen this place before, wherever it was.

I was not in my hotel room, that was for sure. I could see well enough once I got my wits back and my eyes open, but I sure didn't know what it was that I was looking at.

I was in a tiny-bitty little room barely big enough to contain the iron bed I was lying in along with a side table that held a lamp, a leather-bound book and a glass of water. The lamp was not burning, and what light there was came through a very small window set high up on the wall to my right. There was a closed door in the wall to my left. The wall in front of me had a calendar tacked to it. Last year's dates, but the picture on it, some kind of flowers, was pretty so that's probably why they kept it.

Whoever *they* were. I couldn't see or hear anyone.

Something else I couldn't do was to get my mind off that glass of water. My mouth felt so dry I half expected to feel cactus spines growing there, and I couldn't remember wanting anything quite so bad as I wanted a sip of that water. Did I say a sip? A barrel of it would've been more to my liking.

But then it didn't much matter whether I wanted the sip or the hogshead. One seemed about as likely as the other.

I tried to roll onto my side enough to reach for the glass, and that was a mistake.

A lance of agony burned through my chest and the whole right side of my body. I opened my mouth to scream but don't know if I had time enough to get any noise out. Next thing I knew the world was going away again, and I guess I must've passed out.

I woke up to the smell of chicken soup. Wrinkled my nose. Sniffed. Decided it wasn't chicken soup after all, but whatever it was smelled mighty good. I opened my eyes.

"Hello."

She smiled. Oh my. It was the same girl I'd seen before when I was on my way into town. I'd thought she was pretty that day when she was bundled neck-deep in coat and sweater or whatever? I hadn't seen the half of it. She was even prettier now that she wasn't carrying quite so much weight of cloth on her.

Oh, I don't mean she was dressed indecent. Nothing at all like that. She was wearing an ordinary gingham house-dress that buttoned high to the throat and had sleeves down to her wrists, so she was covered all up. She wore an apron over the dress, and her hair was done up in a proper bun. But I could see now how slim and pretty she was and how graceful she moved.

And she had a voice as soft as eiderdown. And a smile fit to melt mountains.

"H'lo." It came out pretty much a croak, my throat being parched and my voice unused in . . . I hadn't no idea for how long. Unused of late, that was for sure.

"Are you hungry?" she asked.

"Starvin'."

She perched on the side of my bed—too far away for me to feel the warmth from her but close enough that I wished I could—and held a bowl and spoon out close to my chin. I don't know where the moisture came from, but my mouth sure commenced to water when she did that.

She spooned up some of what looked like a thin, brownish broth and surveyed the situation for a few seconds, then frowned and returned the spoon to the bowl.

"You aren't gonna . . . ?"

"Of course I am, but let me prop you up a little first. Otherwise I'll spill it all over you."

I was so anxious to get some of that inside me that I wouldn't of cared if I had to wear the rest of it, but I didn't want to come right out and say so, so I kept my mouth shut and left be for a moment.

The girl set the bowl down, lifted up the back of my head—oh my, but she did smell nice—and plumped the pillow underneath my neck. She eased me down again and took up the bowl and spoon for the second time.

I'd thought the broth smelled good? I hadn't known what good was. Not until I got a taste of it. Beef broth it was, rich and aromatic and flavored with itty bits of onion and carrot and I don't know what else.

"That's the best soup I ever tasted," I told her between spoonfuls.

"It will make you feel better."

"It already has." And that was the natural truth too. I could feel the warmth spread deep in my belly better than a shot of whiskey could do. Warmth and strength and . . . hope, maybe. I dunno. I surely felt better with half a bowl of beef broth in me.

I smiled and tried to thank her, but again I'm not real sure if I had time to actually make any sounds before I drifted away into the pain-free healing place.

TWENTY-TWO

"**W**hat"—I opened, swallowed, gave her a moment to withdraw the spoon—"is your name?"

She smiled, dipped the spoon into the soup and fed me another mouthful. "Sarah."

I tried to nod and managed to dribble some soup—we were back to chicken, and it tasted every bit as good as it smelled—onto my chin. Sarah put the soup aside and took up a cloth. She wiped my chin and smiled again.

"Nice name," I said.

"Sarah is the name of Abraham's wife, you know."

I frowned. "Abraham. I don't remember meeting him."

For some reason that made her laugh. "Apparently not," she said. And fed me some more of the chicken soup. It was mighty good. Had rice in it along with some other stuff.

"You have a," I took another mouthful, "last name, I suppose."

"Goodson," she said. She pulled a scrap off a chunk of wheat bread and sopped that in the soup for a moment, then fed it to me. It was marvelous. "My father is Carl Goodson. I know you haven't met him yet either. He told me so. Papa is the town barber, which is as close as we come to having a doctor." She tilted her head to the side and gave me a short looking over, then added, "Papa is also the town preacher."

"Two jobs," I said.

"He only gets paid for the barbering. He says it wouldn't be right to take money for the preaching."

"You sound like you don't necessarily agree with that."

She fed me some more bread dunked in chicken soup.

"How did I," back to the spoon again, "come to be here?"

"You don't remember?"

I shook my head. That didn't result in quite so much pain as it had when I first started waking up. It still hurt. But not so bad I couldn't stand it. Either I was starting to heal just a little or else I was learning to accept agony as being normal.

"John Callum heard a gunshot and went out to see who was shooting. He found you lying in the snow. He and some of the other men carried you to Papa's shop. He took care of you there. Since he didn't know you, he asked about you. They said you were staying at the hotel. Which was fine except they wouldn't be able to take care of you there. No one else seemed to really know you, so Papa had them bring you here."

"This is your home?"

She nodded and took advantage of the break in conversation to feed me the last of the soup. "It's behind the church. Do you remember?"

I nodded. Sure did. I didn't think I would ever forget how pretty she looked that day. Although in truth she looked even prettier to me now. I didn't say anything about that, of course.

"Papa had them bring your things from the hotel too. It's all right here, Mr. Tanner."

"Marshall," I corrected. "George Marshall."

Sarah laughed again. "I'm sorry, Mr. Tanner. Really I am. But it's too late to claim that now. Everybody in town knows who you really are."

Not if she was calling me Tanner, they didn't. But naturally I didn't say that out loud either. "How'd they, um . . . ?"

"Some of the gentlemen already knew who you are, or so I understand. You shouldn't blame them, though. They didn't say anything. It was your credentials that gave you away. They saw them when they were packing up your things to bring over here."

I guess I still looked pretty blank.

"From the hotel?" she tried again but this time kind of tentative in her tone of voice.

Me, I remained blank. Credentials? I had no idea what she was talking about.

"In your saddlebags. Don't you remember?"

"I . . . don't seem to remember as much as I ought to," I said. Which was the natural truth if not exactly all of it.

"Your badge and the letter of introduction. Don't you remember where you put them? They were in your saddlebags. I hope you aren't angry. No one meant to invade your privacy. And you really hadn't hidden them very well."

Badge. *Badge!* What badge? Whatever in the world was this girl saying?

"I think . . . I'd like to go to sleep again now," I told her.

Sarah gathered up her tray with the empty bowl on it and the bread and napkin and stuff. She smiled at me, then hesitated for a moment.

"Yes?"

"I was wondering," she said, "if I should call you Mr. Tanner? Or Marshall?"

"Marshall," I said with a smile. "By all means, do call me Marshall." After all, this was a girl I liked being on first-name basis with.

She smiled again and nodded and carried the tray away, closing the bedroom door behind her so as to give me some privacy.

I shut my eyes and gave thought to getting some more sleep.

Then found my eyes popping wide open as I realized what it was she'd been saying there.

They weren't calling me Marshall by name, danggit.

It was Marshal by *title*.

My dead twin must've been some kind of dang lawman.

And wasn't that just a hoot and a half, by gum.

Me. Being taken for a marshal.

I think I might've laughed myself sick. If I hadn't already taken a bullet in the back so that laughing wasn't a real good idea right now.

TWENTY-THREE

Now, I can be about as dumb as anybody. But it didn't take me extra long to work out in my mind that I didn't really want anybody here in this town to know that I wasn't some marshal named Tanner.

There was only one thing that I knew for absolute certain sure about this Tanner fellow. And that was that the man was dead.

It seemed pretty likely that I was the only person who did know that he was dead.

And I didn't want anybody coming to the conclusion that I was the fellow who'd gone and made him dead.

I mean, here I was, wandering around with his horse and saddle and credentials—which I had yet to see but was willing to accept the girl's word for—and his money in hand, and him laying out there dead on the hard, cold ground somewhere north of town.

If it came out that I wasn't him . . . and that the real Marshal Tanner was cold meat . . . well, I wouldn't hardly blame folks for jumping to the obvious conclusions.

Furthermore, I've done an awful lot of things in my time that were outside the law. Truth is, I've pretty much specialized my whole adult life in doing stuff outside the exact letter of the law. Outside the spirit of it too. Heck, I've busted the beejabbers out of just about every law there is.

Just about. But not quite all.

You see, like I already said, I ain't extra-special bright, but I'm not noted for suicidal stupidity either.

And killing lawmen is a downright sure way to get other lawmen peeved.

Same reason why any professional robber will turn himself inside out to avoid shooting folks down.

You rob a bank, and there's always a bunch of fellows willing to sign on to the posse. After all, riding posse generally pays a couple dollars and all a man can drink. It's fun. I've done it myself a time or two when it wasn't me being chased.

But a posseman's heart is into the fun of the thing and the free whiskey, not vengeance.

After all, the guys they're after have just robbed a bank, that's all. And the general view of things is that it's the bank's money that's been taken. The bank or some insurance company back east will make the loss good, and if the bank robbers get away, well, that's no skin off good ol' Joe Posseman's nose.

What I mean to say is, chasing guys with a posse isn't personal. It's more . . . social, you might say. A fun ride, larruping through the bushes, riding fast and waving guns and talking tough. But it just isn't personal.

Which means that once the chase isn't fun anymore, old Joe the posseman will turn around and go home to mama and the cow that needs milking.

Until or unless the robbers are stupid enough to shoot somebody down.

Now, that makes it personal, if you see what I mean.

Rob from a brick bank building, and the posse is chasing you for the sport of it.

Shoot Joe's brother Bob and the pursuit becomes a whole 'nuther matter.

And the better liked the dead man was, the harder that posse is gonna come and the longer they're gonna stay on the trail.

While I don't mean to pat my own back, when it comes to being a robber—and certain other things as well—I consider myself pretty dang good.

Furthermore, it had been my intention to stay on the job.

Okay, I'd had a few misgivings of late. Thought about going to Mexico. Even thought about going to work for a living.

But one thing I have *not* given fond thought to is the idea of being nailed for murdering a lawman. That sort of unpleasantness generally leads to ugly things like ropes and scaffolds and other such things that I prefer not to dwell upon.

What I concluded real quick whilst I was laying in that bed there was that for as long as I was here in . . . wherever it was I was here in . . . for as long as I was here, I was just gonna have to be this Marshal Tanner.

Whoever he'd been. And whatever it was he'd wanted.

That conclusion did not make for a restful sleep afterward, let me tell you. Nossir, not a bit of it.

TWENTY-FOUR

"Is there a local newspaper?" I asked.

"Nothing printed here, if that's what you mean," the Reverend Carl Goodson told me. Sarah's papa was a nice man in his late forties or thereabouts, balding and bespectacled with fuzzy side-whiskers as if to make up for what he was losing on top. I liked him. Especially so because he played a really lousy game of gin. Overall I was up on him by a couple thousand points, and the number kept growing.

"We get papers in from Austin and San Antonio, sometimes from El Paso too. Is there something in particular you want to see?"

Yeah, there was. Something that would tell me the name of this town where I'd come so close to being buried. But if there was no local paper, well, I already knew what they'd named San Antonio. And knew that this wasn't it.

"No," I told my friendly host. "Just curious about things in general."

"I keep a good supply of back issues over at the shop," Goodson said. Of course he would. I doubt I've ever seen a barbershop that didn't have something lying around to read. "I'll ask Sarah to bring some to you. Would any of them in particular appeal to you?"

"Austin," I said on the theory that something out of the state capital would likely be of interest to a marshal. Besides, I seemed to recall the mayor mentioning that I was recognized because somebody—the bartender? I couldn't for sure recall now—was supposed to've seen me one time in Austin. So if I was gonna have an interest in a city in Texas, then Austin should be as good as any and better than most. "Yes, sir," I said, "if you have some papers from Austin, that would be real nice."

"I'll try to remember that," Carl said. He peered close at his hand, touched one card as if to pull it out, then shifted over to the other end of the fan of cards and plunked the six of clubs down.

"Gin," I told him and showed my cards.

Carl groaned. And began counting.

It was a good thing we weren't playing for money or the man might've come to regret taking me in and saving my life like he done.

TWENTY-FIVE

"Good Lord, Mrs. Goodson, that's the finest meal I've had since, well, since I last sat at my own mother's table." I wiped my mouth and folded the napkin careful and laid it down beside my plate. "You surely do know how to make a body feel better."

"It's nice to see you up and around again, Marshal," the lady said. She acted prim and polite, like the compliment didn't mean anything, but I knew better. Compliments are always welcome, never mind the playacting at modesty.

Sarah's mother was stretching the truth a little when she said I was "up and around," though. It had taken Sarah on one side and Carl on the other to help me get from the bedroom all the way out to the dining table.

Worth the trip, though, I did have to say. Until now Sarah'd been bringing me soups and mashed potatoes and soft stuff like that. This meal, I'd been able to lay into both the fried chicken legs on the platter—I hoped it wasn't anybody else's favorite like that piece always has been mine—and some crusty bread all slathered thick with sweet butter, and some other stuff that Sarah hadn't been letting me close to up until now. My belly felt tick-full at this point. Much more of this and I'd be strong enough maybe to get around some on my own.

"More milk, Marshal?" Mrs. Goodson offered, lifting the pitcher and holding it ready.

"No, ma'am. Thank you." I hadn't the heart to tell her that I detest milk. It tastes nasty to me, kind of smoky and like it's spoiled even when it's still warm from the cow. Mrs. Goodson for some reason had it in mind that milk was sovereign for healing a hurt, and she and Sarah had been doing their best to pour it into me right from the get-go.

Which had been . . . I counted back . . . the better part of two weeks since I'd first woke up in the Goodsons' spare bedroom.

"Would you have some cake, Marshal?"

"Thank you, ma'am, but I'm full to the top." I patted the napkin beside my plate again to show that I was done eating. The truth was that I might've been able to handle a little dessert if it'd been, say, some of that pie like they served over at the cafe. But Mrs. Goodson, fine woman that she was and a good cook too for most things, she just wasn't a very good baker. I'd tried her cakes before a couple times when Sarah was still having to prop me up and feed me like some dang baby, and those cakes were dry and tasteless, and by now I knew better than to take any. "I surely do thank you, though. All of you. I know money can't repay all the kindness you've showed to me here, but I have a little cash in hand. I'd count it a privilege if you'd let me buy some groceries for the household at the very least."

"It has been our pleasure to share God's bounty with a needful Samaritan, Marshal," Carl said, waving the suggestion aside.

"Are you ready to go back to your room, Marshal?" Sarah asked.

Actually I was. I would've expected to be more interested in sitting in the parlor like a regular person for a change, but in fact this going out to the table and sitting upright through a whole meal had taken the starch right out of me. I was feeling limp and shaky and had no stomach for sitting up with the family any longer.

"Here, let me help you. Papa, take his other arm, will you?"

Amongst the three of us we got me onto my feet again and into the bedroom.

Now that I was on my own pins, wobbly though they were, I could see there was a sort of low, padded bench at the foot of the bed, down low enough that I hadn't been able to spot it before even when I was propped up into a sitting position.

Somebody, Sarah or her mother I supposed, had taken all my things—mine and Tanner's—out of the saddlebags, washed and folded everything and laid it out all neat and nice atop the bench. I could see the saddlebags on the floor underneath the bench and the thick bedroll—Tanner's sougan and my own thin blankets put together—under there too.

What interested me the most was that on top of the clothing they'd laid the black leather folder that I'd taken to hold a picture of the dead guy's wife. Now I had to figure that it was a wallet because I'd gone through everything else the man had on him when I came to inherit his gear and I sure hadn't come across any badge or "credentials," whatever those were, at the time. So anything Sarah saw, that I didn't, pretty much had to be inside that folder.

"I'm not quite ready to lie down, if you don't mind," I told my faithful helpers. "I'd like to just set on the side of the bed there for a spell. When I'm ready, I can pull my feet up by myself."

"I don't believe you should try to do that. You're still weak. You can sit here and read if you like, or whatever, but when you're ready to lie down, please call. One of us will come make sure you're all right."

"Thank you, miss. You're mighty kind."

She smiled at me—Lordy, but I did like it when that girl smiled—and motioned for her father to help turn me around and get me perched on the side of the bed.

The borrowed nightshirt I was wearing was already too short, Carl not being quite so tall as me, and I was uncomfortably aware that my ankles, hair and bone and all, were on display, but Sarah didn't seem to notice. Which of course was the polite thing for her to do. I certainly didn't mean to embarrass her any.

The two of them got me situated about as comfortable as I could expect to get, then went out and shut the door so I'd have some privacy, like if I needed the thunder mug or something.

What I wanted wasn't that, though. Soon as they were gone, I began scooting and scooching down along the side of the bed, wiggling my way south to the foot and that black leather wallet.

There was an awful lot more about this Tanner fellow that I needed to know before I went and got well.

Because, you see, there were a few things that I wanted to do *after* I got well.

I'd been thinking about those things, the plans that were kinda growing a bit at a time, pretty nigh the whole time I'd been awake in this bed.

What I needed now in order to make it possible was some more knowledge and I figured that wallet would be the best place to start learning.

TWENTY-SIX

Riley. Now, what the heck kinda name was Riley? Irish maybe? I wasn't sure. But hey, that was me. Now.

Riley B. Tanner, that's what the paper said. Deputy United States Marshal Riley B. Tanner. It didn't say what the B stood for.

There was a badge inside the wallet, all right. A round, silver one with parts of the metal cut away to make a star inside the circle and in the middle of the star the one word "Marshal" and around the outside of the circle the much smaller words "Department of Justice" at the top and "United States of America" at the bottom. Impressive.

It was the paper folded up and kept in the opposite compartment of the wallet that was more helpful to me, though. Most of it was printed with a few particulars filled in with ink in a flowery but legible handwriting. The paper was a commission declaring Riley B. Tanner to be a sworn and duly authorized—whatever that meant—officer of the court representing the United States Department of Justice, Office of the Attorney General. Huh. A general, no less.

It wasn't signed by a general but by a judge, one Eustace Fairbanks, Jr. It didn't say where his court was. His handwriting was real nice.

More helpful, and likely of more use to me, several possibilities coming to mind right off, was a paper that had

been tucked in behind the deputy's commission. That one
was a To Whom It May Concern thing, also signed by a
federal judge but this one named Robert J. Talbot, confirm-
ing that Deputy Marshal Riley B. Tanner was engaged in
activities for and under the direction of the United States
judiciary, and asking any and all parties to cooperate with
Deputy Marshal Tanner in the completion of his tasks.

The commission paper was dated more than a year ago.
Judge Talbot's letter was dated less than a month back. It
didn't say just what tasks everybody was supposed to help
Tanner complete.

Which I suppose was just as well. I might've felt bad
about ignoring those instructions if I'd known what they
were. Sure I would've. You bet.

I took everything out of the wallet, even the badge itself
which didn't have one of those flimsy pin-and-latch ar-
rangements on the back of it like you might expect but had
two pointy little posts on the back and wide, flat screws
that fit over them to hold the badge in place on a shirt or
a vest or in this case a flap of thin, very fine leather.

I'd seen an awful lot of badges in my time but never
from the back side or quite this close up, and I found it
sort of interesting. I don't know why.

Anyhow, I'd maybe have done things different right from
the get-go if I'd had sense enough to take a thorough look
inside the wallet back when I first could. So I made up for
the oversight this time and examined it every which way
short of undoing the stitching and taking it apart.

The badge and the two papers were all it held, though.

Which was enough. At least it told me who I was and
who my boss was. That was more than I'd known before.

Riley.

I'd never known anyone named Riley before. Might have
found it easier to get used to if the dead guy'd been named
Bill or Tom or Jim, something regular and natural.

Still, if anybody hollered out to tell a Riley to duck, I
guessed I'd know it would be me they meant and could go
about the business of getting out of the way without looking
into details.

It would have been nice if somebody'd yelled for Riley to duck a couple weeks ago.

But if they had, I wouldn't have known it was me that was supposed to duck, would I?

Besides, among the very few things that I've managed to learn in the pursuit of a mostly happy, even if somewhat misspent, lifetime is that complaining about the past or playing games with the words "what if" darn seldom prove worth the bother and the time invested.

Because no matter how bitter your tears, you aren't gonna make any part of yesterday change, so you might just as well go ahead and put your thinking toward tomorrow and the rest of today.

At least, that's what Deputy Marshal Riley B. Tanner would advise. I was sure of it. If you don't believe it, why, just ask me, because I was dang sure him.

TWENTY-SEVEN

Now, I got to admit that I was not keeping a close accounting, but as near as I can figure it by the time I was able to get around more or less normal the Reverend Barber Carl Goodson owed me something in the neighborhood of $1,200 in gin losses. It could have been more, but like I said I wasn't keeping real close track of it.

The good thing is that I wasn't really expecting him to cough up hard cash, seeing as we'd been playing for fun and not for serious. The amazing thing to me was that him and his missus wouldn't accept any kind of payment for all they'd done for me.

Those two people—and Sarah; Lordy, I couldn't forget Sarah—had saved my life. And in this particular case that is not no figure of speech; it is a literal truth. I would've died for sure back then, either facedown in the snow when it happened or slowly and even more painful over a period of time after, if it hadn't been for the care I got in the Goodson home.

I got to admit that I felt bad about lying to the Goodsons. Which in a way I guess I went and did by letting them think I was Deputy U.S. Marshal Riley B. Tanner.

On the other hand, every time I got to feeling sorrowful about that fact, I made myself ponder just what was apt to happen should I let the cat outa the bag and admit to who I really was.

Wasn't no way this side of the pearly gates that anyone would take my unsupported story for what happened, and the most likely upshot of the misunderstanding would be that I would end up hanging for the murder of the real Marshal Tanner.

No, that didn't sit too well whenever I thought on it, so I bit my lip, steeled my resolve and kept my big mouth shut about my true identity.

Of course . . . it didn't hurt my feelings any once I reached that conclusion to know that I had a whole lot better chance of getting Sarah Goodson to take an interest in me by being Riley Tanner than I would if I went and piped up with something on the order of, "Oh, by the way, miss, I'm not really the fine, upstanding peace officer you think I am but instead am wanted for assorted crimes an' misdemeanors in several states and territories. But let's just forget about that and how's about you let me squire you to the after-church dinner social come next Sunday?"

That would go over big, I'm sure. With Sarah, with her mama, with the Reverend Barber Goodson, heck with the whole darn town.

Which I *still* didn't know the name of, seeing as I still hadn't been able to think up a logical reason or way to ask anybody about it.

It was a vexation to me, let me tell you. Albeit not as much of one as certain other things that I also didn't know. Yet.

Anyway, once I put my mind to it, I got about the business of healing fairly quick, everything considered, and in less than a month felt I was steady enough to walk outside on my own hind legs.

TWENTY-EIGHT

Texas looked different now than I remembered it being. Last time I was outdoors there was snow. Lots of it. Now you'd think it was springtime and never mind the calendar. The sun was warm and the sky clear and the air gentle on my cheeks. It felt mighty good to stand outside on the porch of the Reverend Barber Goodson's place and look at something other than walls.

I hadn't actually planned on taking a walk. I was still weak and shaky. My legs felt like they were made of straw, and it was kind of hard for me to breathe. Carl said he was pretty sure one of my lungs had been punctured by the bullet and that it would take the longest to completely heal.

You couldn't say that I was exactly back to good health, but of a sudden the sky and the fresh air seemed so good that I just wanted to be out away from that house for a little while.

The Reverend Barber Goodson and his family had been wonderful to me. Sarah especially. So that wasn't it. I just . . . wanted to be someplace else, and on my own, if only for a couple minutes.

There was a handrail built beside the four stone steps down from the porch to the walk, so I took hold of it and made my way slow and careful down to the ground. I hadn't had to do any such thing in . . . Come to think of it,

I couldn't recall ever having to hold onto anything like that before, not ever, but I felt the need for it now. I didn't trust either my strength or my balance, but now that I'd decided, I was bound to make it out to the street and around the block at the very least. I was set on that, and I admit that I can be on the stubborn side sometimes. I eased my way down, took a deep breath and set out for I didn't know where. But slow. Slow and cautious.

I was around the corner and halfway down the block before it occurred to me that I'd come outside wearing nothing but my clothes.

That is, I'd left my guns, my own and the dead man's, back in the Goodson house.

That wasn't an extra smart thing for me to've done, considering that the last time I took a stroll somebody shot me in the back.

It wasn't beyond reason to think that whoever it was that missed killing me the first time—well, missed killing Marshal Tanner, as that would be the way they'd be seeing it—just might want to try and get it right in a repeat of that first encounter. First encounter or second, actually. It had occurred to me, while I was lying on my back with nothing better to do than think, that it surely could be that I'd been shot at twice here in this no-name town, the first time being that scattering of gunfire from far down the street that I'd taken to be some idiot drunks who didn't know what they were doing.

It just could be that they'd known exactly what they were doing. But not how to do it.

Shooting from long range with a short gun isn't sensible. Not if a fellow is serious. But then not too awful many folks have actual experience when it comes either to shooting at other folks or to being shot at their own selves.

With the gunfire greenhorns, it can be a lot like taking a kid on his first hunt. Buck fever isn't just some name plucked out of nowhere. It's real for a good many first-time hunters. They can get so excited about the thought of bringing down that fat buck out there that they shake and tremble and don't hardly know what they're doing. I've seen youngsters shoot everything from treetops to the ground right spang in front of them when they get that first crack at a big whitetail.

The good thing for them but maybe bad for me is that buck fever usually isn't a permanent condition. Experience tends to make it go away.

And if the boys who'd been shooting at me had had buck fever that first time, they seemed to've near about conquered it in the second attempt. Enough so to put lead into me anyway. It was pure luck that kept that bullet in my lungs from killing me.

I didn't think I could count on luck, or Sarah Goodson and her papa, saving me a second time.

Much as I was enjoying my walk in the sunshine, I started to feel real naked with nothing around my waist except my britches.

I turned around and tottered straight on back to the Goodson house there on the edge of whatever the heck this town was.

TWENTY-NINE

Over the next couple days I found that I was able to walk further and easier as the healing progressed. And I found too that I was a heckuva lot more comfortable outdoors now when I had a revolver strapped at my hip.

It wasn't very easy for me to adjust to that, actually. Most folks think that just because a person does things for a living that most people frown on—you know, robbing banks and stagecoaches and like that—that he wears a gun all the time and probably kicks stray dogs too.

The truth is that while a peace officer may have to wear a gun all the time, my kind don't.

Think about it. A lawman never knows when he might could run into trouble, but a robber picks and chooses the times he feels like working.

And guns, danggit, are heavy and uncomfortable things to wear.

They drag your pants down on one side so that you have to wear suspenders in addition to the gunbelt or anyway a belt separate from the belt you have the holster and cartridges on. And even then there is always that weight pulling and twisting and annoying a person. It isn't comfortable.

And if you wear them, they get dirty. Wet and dusty and

full of grit, so then you have to clean them twice as often as you otherwise might.

They're an invitation to trouble too. Go out for a drink of an evening, and the guy standing next to you may have himself a snootful. Well, if you have a gun on your hip, that sort of thing can lead to misunderstandings and various sorts of trouble and even to the pissed-off kind of posse that I mentioned before. Like if you wind up shooting some idiot. Which at that is better than standing there and being shot *by* that same idiot. And believe me, I know what I'm talking about there. In my younger, tomfoolery days I've had it both ways. Been shot and done the shooting both. Trust me. It's better to be the one that does the shooting. It's a whole lot more fun running from a posse than healing from a wound, as I was lately reminded.

Yet experience has also shown me that if you go out drinking and the only thing you're carrying on your hip is a handkerchief, then no one, not even the drunk beside you, expects you to take a hand in any serious nastiness. All you got to do on those evenings is make sure you're out of the line of fire from all the young jehus who haven't yet learned to leave their guns wrapped up in an oily cloth somewhere while they go out for an evening of refreshment and good times.

All of which hard-won knowledge, of course, did me no good now since it wasn't some overwrought drunk that already tried to put me under but a . . . well, I didn't know what or who or why somebody wanted me dead before and could be safely presumed to still hold that unpleasant notion.

Point was, I couldn't sashay about making any assumptions when it came to the peaceful goodwill of my fellow man. I was better off thinking the worst of just about everybody I passed on the street, as any one among them could've been the party who came so close already to settling my hash.

So as Deputy Marshal Riley B. Tanner I saw to the cleanliness of my old .44–40 Colt and to that of the much newer—higher serial number—but otherwise pretty nigh identical single-action Peacemaker that'd been carried by the late Mr. Tanner.

I strapped my own tried and true gun on and for good measure dropped the spare into my coat pocket.

Once that was done, I felt better equipped to face the world beyond the walls of the Goodson residence.

THIRTY

Now, I know approximately doodah when it comes to figuring out who did what to who. Whom? Who. I dunno. Point is, I consider myself a better than merely fair hand when it comes to *doing* a crime . . . but I don't know diddly about investigating one.

You would think that two sides of one coin would be close enough to the same that if you were familiar with one, you ought to be able to work out the other. Well, it isn't that way. Heck, look at a coin, any coin. Turn it over. The two sides are completely different, right? And that's the same thing I was finding out now that I was trying to think up ways to learn who'd tried to murder me from ambush.

The real Marshal Tanner might've found this deal to be a snap. But I wasn't him, and I didn't know how to properly go about a criminal investigation.

Which, of course, is what this thing had become.

I mentioned, I think, that I'd been stewing about some stuff while I was lying in that bed being spoon-fed by Sarah Goodson. And what I'd been coming down to—okay, I mean what I'd been thinking about other than Sarah and how awfully pretty she was—what I'd been coming to was a deep down, slow burning mad.

Some miserable SOBs, for reasons I couldn't even begin to guess at, tried to kill me.

Never mind that they thought they were gunning down Riley B. Tanner.

It was me that took the bullet in the back, me that laid there week after week in misery, me that still was walking wobbly and slow because of it.

And by golly it was me that was now purely pissed off by the deal.

I had me a badge and, at least as far as anybody around here knew, legal authority to go hunting for whoever it was that shot me.

Well, I was gonna do it.

Twice now they'd tried to put me under. Twice I'd survived being taken like a lamb to slaughter.

Well now the lamb was gonna turn into a mean and feisty old ram and do some fighting back.

Somebody might could put me down. I never claimed to be the baddest man in town, any town. But anybody that takes me will have to work for it. I won't step back and let him have no more free licks.

From here on in, I swore silent to myself, from here on in it was going to be me against them.

And I figured I was going to take it just as hard and just as far as it needed to be took.

I started out with my first order of business trying to find out who-all in this town knew who Riley B. Tanner was, because while I don't know anything about investigating stuff, I wasn't so dumb that I couldn't figure out there was a purpose behind the shootings. Somebody knew and was scared of Deputy Marshal Tanner. Somebody had something they wanted hid, something that Tanner must have known about or would have been expected to find out about.

Somebody.

My question now was: Who?

THIRTY-ONE

"Amos . . . that is your name, i'n it? Amos?"

The fat bartender nodded and reached for a beer mug.

"I don't want a beer just yet, Amos. Right now I'm wanting to have a talk with you."

"I don't know anything, Marshal."

I smiled at him. There's been some folks a time or two in the past that've turned real pale when I've gone and smiled at them. Usually when I've also been holding a gun on them, but the gun part isn't always strictly necessary. It's a point I can generally get across when I want to. "I still want us to have that talk, Amos. Just you and me."

The fat man looked this way and that, but there wasn't anybody else in the saloon. Which of course was why I'd come at this early hour. I wanted a mite of privacy. "I don't know anything, Marshal. Honest."

"And I'm sure you are telling me the truth." I paused and frowned just the least bit. "You *are* going to tell me nothing but the truth aren't you, Amos?"

"Yes, sir. Of course I am."

"That's nice, Amos. I appreciate it. I really do." I smiled a little, and Amos began to look more than just a little bit apprehensive.

I crooked my finger to beckon the man closer. He picked

up a bar towel and began nervously twisting and turning it in his hands, but he came over to stand where I indicated.

"Now, Amos, I remember how you told Mayor Tolliver and his friends who I am. D'you remember that day, Amos?"

He nodded. He looked like he had a bad taste in his mouth, but he nodded.

"Now the thing I need to know, Amos, is who *else* you told."

Amos shook his head. Quick and vigorous. "Nobody, Marshal. I swear it. I didn't tell it to anybody else."

I smiled real big at him. Practically beamed with happiness and slapped the surface of the bar while my grin just got bigger and bigger.

"Now, Amos," I said, "I am pleased to hear that, because that means that it's surely one of those three gentlemen that twice tried to shoot me down. Has to be one of them, see, because they're the only ones that knew who I really was, right?" Of course it didn't necessarily follow that if the one thing was true then the other had to be also. Heck, for all I knew—or for all Amos knew—half the population could've previously known and recognized Riley Tanner here. But I wasn't much inclined to give ol' Amos time to work that part of it out for himself.

"I expect I can just place all three of them under arrest and let the court work out who's guilty and how many of them were in on it. I can count on your testimony come that time, can't I, Amos? That the only three men you told about me was . . . let me think back . . . It was the mayor, of course. And Sheriff Frake. And the third man at the table that day was the banker Mr. Carlton. Excuse me, I mean Mr. Brainard. Carlton is his first name not his last, isn't that right?"

"No!" the fat man yelped.

I frowned again. "Carlton isn't his first name?"

"No, I mean, yes, I mean . . . Mr. Carlton Brainard owns the bank. But I didn't . . ."

"You did tell him and Mayor Tolliver and Sheriff Frake who I was, Amos. That's right, isn't it?"

"Yes, but . . ."

"And you say you didn't tell anybody else. That's right too, isn't it, Amos? So therefore them . . . and you, of course . . . they're the only ones knew who I was." My frown got real serious. "Unless you're the one shot at me. I hadn't actually thought about that before this minute, Amos. It could've been you that shot me in the back. Attempted murder, Amos. Assault on a United States deputy marshal. That's serious stuff, Amos. Put you away for a real long time for something like that. You'd be an old man by the time you got out. If you lived long enough to get out, that is." I shrugged. "You never know about that. Hard place, prison. Real hard."

Amos was sweating now.

"I never . . . Mr. Brainard, he wouldn't . . . Look, Marshal, uh . . . it could be . . . I mean I don't remember for sure, you understand . . . but I might have, well, you know."

"No, Amos, I don't know. That's why I came here today." I turned the frown into a smile again. "So's you and me could have us a private talk. You know?"

"I maybe . . . That is to say that it could be." He stopped, took a deep breath. "I just might have let it slip out to a couple other fellows who you really were, Marshal."

"Uh huh. And who might those particular fellows have been, Amos? You think on this real hard before you answer. Because you might have to testify to all this under oath. You know what I mean?"

"Yes, sir. I . . . I'll try and think of anybody else. Honestly I will."

"That's nice, Amos. Now, while you're thinking, you can draw me a beer. Just a short one, hear. Then you and me can finish this friendly little chat. Would that be all right?"

He mopped his face with the bar towel—which showed more courage than I would of had; that thing looked awful dirty—and looked relieved.

"I'll . . . Just give me a second to get your beer, Marshal. I'm sure I can remember who all I might have talked to that afternoon."

"You do that, Amos. You just do that."

I accepted the beer he put in front of me but did not reach into my pocket for the usual nickel. After all, how many times had I seen coppers and night marshals stand around drinking on the house. I would have to say that I got kind of a kick out of doing the same thing now my own self.

THIRTY-TWO

Bluff and bluster. That's what it came down to. I'd bluffed poor old Amos and blustered and more or less threatened—I didn't feel very good about that part of it—and all I'd come away with was more questions than there were answers.

He'd said he thought he might've mentioned about my identity—that is, about dead-and-gone Riley Tanner's identity—to a couple cowboys that afternoon.

The fellows I'd seen in here at the time? No, not them, he'd thought. They'd left, or so he recalled it to've been, but some other boys dropped in during the afternoon, hands drifting by to warm their bellies from the inside out, and, well, it was just maybe possible that he *might* have mentioned to one or two of them that he'd seen a deputy marshal in the place and, yeah, he could have commented too that this deputy wasn't wanting folks in town—Lordy, I did wish he'd of said the name of the town when he got to that part—that the deputy wasn't owning up to who he was or why it might be he was here.

Who had those riders been? I'd asked him.

Couldn't recall for sure, Amos swore. One fellow who went by the name of Ike, he thought but wasn't positive. He couldn't remember the others. If there'd been any others.

Amos was a big help. Sure.

I asked him what outfit these fellows rode for, thinking that could give me a direction to look in.

Amos just shrugged. He only saw their faces, he told me. Once in a while he'd hear their names. Unless somebody rode his horse inside, which was against the house rules, he wouldn't have occasion to read their brands.

I supposed that sounded reasonable enough. Disappointing, but reasonable.

I thought about trying to squeeze Amos some more, then reconsidered. It wasn't like I could exactly afford to push him too far, so that the man would get his back up and start to sull.

Heck, if he or for that matter anybody else around here decided to call my bluff, what was I supposed to do? Put them behind bars? I wouldn't know how.

And I'd sure feel silly as all billy blue hell trying to do it.

The very few times I'd enjoyed some town's hospitality my own self I hadn't been sober enough to keep track of what was happening outside the cell bars. You know, all the paperwork and mumbo jumbo and stuff that I suppose had to go on.

I knew there was paperwork to it. A fellow saw that in the morning once he sobered up and had to stand before a magistrate to be told off for the fine and a night's jail sentence like was normal. And no, I've never actually been arrested for anything serious. Been chased aplenty but never caught, knock on wood. Drunk and disorderly is about the worst of it, thank goodness, that and a $1 fine once for speeding my horse through town. That was up in Medicine Lodge. Nice town. I've always liked it. And I don't hold the speeding fine against them. I don't think the town marshal would have bothered except there were some high faluting ladies that got dust on their dimples from me running past and complained to the law about me.

I got back at them though. I found out the most vocal and nasty among those women was the daughter of the town's biggest merchant. That man did a good trade, let me tell you. Held quite a bit of money in his safe of a

Saturday night when the receipts were heavy and the bank already closed for the weekend by the time he shut his doors.

Poor fellow. He had money, but his daughter was ugly and his wife even worse. I wouldn't have swapped places with him, that's for sure.

Anyway, I knew better than to think I could step right in now and go to putting folks here in . . . wherever we were . . . behind bars. Any serious mistakes about how a body was supposed to do a thing like that and Sheriff Frake was sure to figure me out. That was not a thing I especially wanted to allow, so I gave up on pestering Amos and finished my beer, dipped lightly into the free lunch spread and headed out to see if I could find another way of sneaking up on this thing.

THIRTY-THREE

The bank! Of course. The bank would be named for the town. All I had to do was find the bank and I'd know what the town was called. I was becoming obsessed with the idea that I needed to know where I was. Well, I had a pretty fair reason for wanting to know, after all. It was something I was sure expected to know, and any slip of the tongue in that regard could expose me for a fraud. So not only did I want to know, I really needed to too.

So I asked a fellow on the street where I could find the bank and hurried right over there.

A big old sign was posted covering the full width of the single-story brick bank building.

Cattlemen's Bank and Trust, C. M. Brainard, Pres.

Yeah, that told me everything I needed to know. Darn it. Still, there was more than just the one reason for me to drop by.

I went inside and kind of chuckled a little to myself when I did. There I was, in broad daylight and with no help nor horse-holders posted outside. No bandanna pulled up over my face nor gun in hand. And there I was, walking into the Cattlemen's Bank and Trust just as bold and sassy as anybody could be. It kind of tickled me.

Kind of tempted me, though, when I got a good look inside the place. There was one mousy-looking teller on duty behind the cash window, and the vault was behind him, a big and impressive-looking floor-to-ceiling safe made by the Henry Jarlsson Co. of Cincinnati, Ohio. Oh my, but I like to started drooling down my own shirtfront.

The thing is, I've had the pleasure of working with Jarlsson products before. They are handsome things, big and expensive. But their innards aren't near so impressive as their outters. So to speak.

I mean, five minutes with a drill and a really good shove with a four-foot pry bar and I could pop the door on that Jarlsson without hardly making a sound. Unless the hinges needed oiling, that is, and a fellow could always remember to bring along an oil can on his way to work.

Good old Henry Jarlsson. I'd never met the man, but I sure was grateful to him.

That wasn't what I'd come here for, though, and I put it out of mind. More or less.

"Yes, sir?" the teller asked.

I smiled at him. Managed to keep myself from giggling but the fellow sure got a big enough smile. Then I made myself get serious. "Mr. Brainard, please."

"I don't . . . Are you a depositor, sir?"

"No, I'm Marshal Tanner. I think you'll find that Mr. Brainard and me have met already."

"I'm sorry, Marshal. Of course, you have. He has mentioned you several times. After your, um, accident?"

"It wasn't no accident. I was shot. From ambush. You did hear it that way, didn't you?"

"Well, um, yes. I suppose that I did."

"Would you just tell Mr. Brainard that I'd like a word with him? Please?"

"Of course, Marshal. One moment, please."

Supercilious little son of a bitch!

Hey, that's a pretty good word, isn't it. Supercilious. I'd read it someplace but never had any occasion to use it before. I thought it was pretty dandy, so much so that I wasn't even peeved with the fellow any longer when he turned to priss on back to a room off to the left of the public part of the bank.

THIRTY-FOUR

Nice man, Mr. Brainard. I liked him. Didn't learn a darn thing from him, but I liked him.

What I was asking, of course, was who-all he might've told about me after we met in the saloon that day.

His answer wasn't particularly helpful. He said he talked about me with George Tolliver and Herb Frake, of course. They were all three at the table that day and were the first ones to hear from the bartender who I "really" was. Which of course I already knew.

Apart from those two gentlemen . . . He scrunched his face into a scowl of deep concentration as he tried to think back . . . He took time enough to think it over a couple, three times, then shook his head.

"I'm sorry, Marshal. I can't think of anyone else. Apart from my wife, that is. I probably mentioned it to her. Edith and I discuss almost everything, so I would assume that I mentioned you to her. Mind now, I don't recall specifically that I did, but it would be unusual for me to neglect passing on something so exciting." He smiled. "Small towns are like that, as you may know. It is boring, plain and simple. Nothing much out of the ordinary ever happens in a place like this, so we talk about any tiny little thing that occurs. It isn't like being in the big cities like you must be used to."

I let that pass as I hadn't any idea where-all Marshal Tanner might've been expected to visit. Or worse, where-all somebody here in—wherever we were—somebody here might know Tanner to've visited. And since I hadn't been very much of anyplace south of the Indian Territories up till now I figured I was best off to keep my mouth shut. Somebody could ask me the name of the main street in Austin, say, and I wouldn't have the least idea how to respond. Main Street? How the heck would I know since I'd never been a step closer to the place than I was right at this very moment.

Anyway, I smiled and nodded and thanked Mr. Brainard for being so helpful. Which he wasn't, but never mind that.

I thanked him and got out of there before he started in on idle chitchat of the sort that could lead to me saying or doing something to draw suspicion to myself.

Besides which, I was still mighty weak from the gunshot wound, which was mostly but not yet entirely healed. I still needed rest in the afternoons, I'd found.

Afternoon naps! Can you imagine? A body would think I was eighty years old and feeble.

And at times I kind of felt like I was.

I thanked Mr. Brainard, ignored the supercilious bank teller—sounded just as good the second time, by gum—and made my way real slow back to the Goodson house out at the edge of town.

Sure did wish I could get a handle on the name of this place, though. I knew I'd feel a whole lot better once I knew where I was.

THIRTY-FIVE

"Ma'am, you've been so good to me, you and everybody else in this family, that I don't hardly know how to thank you for it all. Couldn't repay it with every cent I got. I tell you the truth, ma'am, you and the reverend and Sarah, I just can't begin to tell you how much your kindness has meant to me." I took another mouthful of pot roast so tender a body needn't have teeth in his mouth to chew it. "I expect I'd best be moving back to the hotel now that I'm on my feet again, though," I concluded.

"We'll hear none of that, Marshal," Mrs. Goodson said in a no-nonsense tone of voice.

"We will not," the Reverend Barber Goodson added.

"You aren't fooling us, Marshal," Sarah put in. "We can see how tired you still get after a little bit of walking. You will stay here until you are fully recovered."

"And that is the last we will discuss this, Marshal," Mrs. Goodson said with a sniff and a nod.

"The last," The Reverend Barber Goodson echoed.

"We won't listen to any argument," Sarah said.

"Yes'm," I said to none of them in particular. And reached out to spear another boiled potato. Hang around here much longer and I'd get so fat, old ugly, you wouldn't be able to carry me.

Which reminded me, I was soon going to have to walk

down to the livery and see how my horse—my horses, that is; I'd 'most forgotten Tanner's gray horse, which was also down at the livery eating at my expense—how the two of them were getting along. I supposed I should ante up for the cost of their board too while I was at it. I didn't care all that much about the gray but wouldn't have wanted the liveryman Alex to start short-feeding ugly just because I was too lazy to come in and pay my bill. And thinking of that reminded me . . .

"We haven't talked about my board bill yet," I reminded the Reverend Barber Goodson.

He gave me a funny sort of look. Mrs. Goodson and Sarah stopped eating and looked at me like I was a traveling medicine show exhibit.

"There is no bill," he said.

"Of course not," Mrs. Goodson sniffed.

"You are being quite foolish this evening, Marshal," Sarah said.

"What we have given is simple Christian charity," the reverend said.

"I got money, you know. I don't need charity."

"I did not mean it that way, Marshal," he told me.

"We do not take payment for doing what is right," Mrs. Goodson said.

"You folks saved my life."

"The Lord God saved your life, Marshal."

"We were merely fortunate enough to be His instrument."

"You don't owe us anything."

"We won't talk about this again."

They were all three of them fussing at me at one and the same time so that it was hard for me to know which one to look at or which to duck away from. They sure were sassy on that subject, though.

"You saved my life," I insisted.

"We are happy we could help."

"We expect nothing in return."

"Please, Marshal Tanner. Don't insult Mama and Papa by asking them to take money. The little we've done has been our pleasure." Sarah smiled. Oh my, but that girl

could light up a ballroom from one end to the other with
one tiny smile. I hadn't yet seen a chandelier with candles
enough on it to compare with the brightness of her smile.

"Now, help yourself to the gravy for that potato, Marshal," Mrs. Goodson instructed. "No, don't hold back. Dip
the last out of the boat there. I have more in the kitchen.
Finish that, please, and I'll bring some more. And Sarah.
Pass the marshal the corn if you please. The gentleman's
plate is nigh empty." She smiled, grabbed the newly empty
gravy boat and went off toward the kitchen with a swish
of starched skirts and what looked like a great and fearsome
anxiety that someone at her table might be in danger of
going hungry.

I sighed just a little. But what could I do? I took the corn
that Sarah offered and helped myself to a yeast roll that I
tore in half and used to sop up some of that gravy with.
Lordy, I hadn't eaten this good since I was three or four
years old and fell into the trough with the pigs.

THIRTY-SIX

*B*road Valley. Glory be, I was in Broad Valley, Texas. It said so right there over the post office window. Broad Valley. I was so tickled from coming to know that I could've just spit. Would have too except I was indoors and didn't want to get thrown out of the store until I'd had a chance to do the business that brought me here.

But I really was in a fine good humor of a sudden. Broad Valley, indeed.

I turned back toward the door of the general store—I don't know why I was so dumb that I hadn't thought of finding the post office before now—and took a long look outside.

No, there weren't any mountains that had gone and crept near while I wasn't looking. No mountains, no hills, not even any ridges worth squinting at. So how they'd come to decide that this flat, empty stretch of flat and empty was really a valley, well, I couldn't quite figure that one.

Still, someone sometime did look at this dust wallow and decide to call it Broad Valley, and now I knew that they did, b'golly. I felt so good I like to danced a jig, and I guess I was smiling when I greeted the man in charge of the place.

"Good morning, sir. My name is Tanner, sir. Riley Tanner." Yeah, well, in for a penny, in for a pound, right?

"Oh, I know who you are, Marshal. Everyone in Broad Valley knows that by now, I'm sure."

Huh! Whyn't he rub it in. Now that I already knew the name, *now* somebody was willing to speak it out loud. It was like they somehow knew and were being contrary. I knew that wasn't so, of course. But I kinda felt like it all the same. Not that any of it was this man's fault.

"I'm Horace Yost." He stuck his hand out, and we shook. "What can I do for you, Marshal?"

"I came by to see about buying some stuff," I told him.

"Selling stuff is what I do, so maybe I can help you. Did you have any particular stuff in mind?"

I liked Mr. Yost. There was a sparkle in his eye that showed he wasn't sour and serious like a lot of storekeepers are. Something about them having to stay indoors and work when everybody else is wandering around in the sunshine, I guess. A lot of storekeepers are sourpusses anyway, I can attest to that. But not Mr. Yost.

"I have a problem, Mr. Yost, and I'm hoping you can help me with it."

"If I can, certainly."

"First thing, d'you deliver?" I wasn't in much shape to be hauling and carrying just yet.

"I tell you what, Marshal. If you give me an order for anything more than, oh let's say twenty-five," he paused for half a moment, "cents. Anything above that, I'll see that your stuff is delivered. Is that fair?"

"You drive a hard bargain, Mr. Yost, but I'm game. Twenty-five cents it is." I nodded. "You, uh, did quote me that figure for the entire order, didn't you?"

"Close," he said. "Real close." He laughed.

"The thing is, Mr. Yost, I been staying with the Goodson family. I take it they do shop here, don't they? The Reverend Goodson and his family? They're the ones directed me here when I asked them about a store."

"Carl and Elvira do shop here, yes."

"So you'd be knowing kinda how their tastes run?"

"If you are wanting to ask me questions about the Goodsons' private matters, Marshal . . ."

"No, sir, don't be taking me wrong, please. I don't wanta

know anything. It's just that I been eating their food an' sleeping in their bed an' being about as much of a nuisance as one lone human person can manage for these past weeks now, and they won't any of them take so much as a penny of pay from me for it all.''

"That sounds like them all right," Yost agreed.

"Yeah, well, I can't talk them into taking board money from me, Mr. Yost, but I'm thinking surely they wouldn't refuse was I to stock up their pantry for them. Which is what I'm wanting you to do. I'd like you to make up an order of goods for the family. Whatever they generally buy and lots of it. And throw some extras in too, whatever you think they might like but not normally feel up to buying for themselves. Could you do that for me, Mr. Yost? I'd be beholden.''

The suspicion that had momentarily tightened the muscles at Horace Yost's jaw loosened up and he began smiling bigger than ever. "Marshal, I would be proud to sell you the stuff you asked for. And I'll tell you something else. I won't even charge you full price for all of it. I'll give you what break I can when I calculate the damages. All right?''

"That's plenty all right, Mr. Yost, and I think I'll enjoy doing business with you. Do you want I should leave a deposit for my stuff now?''

The storekeeper—and part-time postmaster, I gathered—shook his head. "No need. Drop by at your convenience, Marshal. I'll have a bill itemized and made out for you. We can settle up then.''

"Thank you, sir. Thank you very much.''

I touched the brim of my hat and went back out onto the street. It was a fine, fair day in Broad Valley, Texas, and I thought the air smelled mighty sweet indeed.

THIRTY-SEVEN

Well, that was easy enough to figure out. Obviously, since practically nobody in Broad Valley, Texas, knew who I was, nobody in Broad Valley, Texas, had any reason to shoot at me.

Therefore, I concluded, nobody shot at me. Simple, right?

Heck, that *had* to be the answer. After all, I'd talked with the bartender, the banker, the sheriff and the mayor. They all swore they hadn't blabbed. Except for Amos, that is, and he claimed he wasn't really sure if he mentioned anything to some cowboy or other and if he did it wasn't like they would of been anybody important.

The banker Mr. Brainard, the mayor Mr. Tolliver and Sheriff Herb Frake all said they were sure they hadn't told anybody, not anybody at all, save maybe for their wives.

And even I couldn't think of any reason why one of the town's ladies would want to gun down a deputy United States marshal, so I was left with the conclusion that I'd probably imagined the whole thing. Maybe some kid threw a rock and that's what put the hole in my back.

This business of looking at crimes from the law-ward end of things was harder than I'd ever given it credit for up to now.

I decided I'd best give it a rest for the moment and think

about other stuff right now. Like my ugly old horse. It was a long walk from the Goodson place out at the east end of town to the livery stable on the west side, and I was already halfway there, so after lunch at the cafe I walked over there, slow so as to save my strength. I was feeling a whole lot better by now and my strength was coming back, but I still had a way to go before I'd call the recovery complete.

Alex, who owned the place, was there when I arrived. So was ugly. The homely old thing looked pretty good considering the fact that he was such a nasty-and-useless-looking critter.

"He looks almost fat," I told Alex.

"Thank you."

I nodded, pleased that he'd understood it was a compliment, for that was what I'd intended. "Thought you might be getting worried about the board bill."

Alex yawned and unpiled himself off the upended bucket he'd been using for a stool. "Not since I heard who you was," he said. "Besides, I've knowed right along where to find you." He showed me a picket fence of yellow teeth with frequent gaps to break up the monotony in his mouth. "If you're going to go around letting people shoot at you, though, it might be good if you was to sign the voucher for me now. That way I can submit it even if you go and get yourself killed unexpected-like."

"Voucher?"

"You didn't bring one? That's all right. I've dealt with the gov'ment before. I have some on hand for just such as this. Wait here a minute."

I nodded and waited. Didn't have the least idea what this man was talking about. But he seemed to. So I nodded like this was all old hat to me and stood there waiting to see what happened.

What happened was that he stepped into the tack room that doubled him for office space and came out a moment later carrying a printed form sort of thing that had some official-looking numbers on it and spaces where information could be filled in. At the top it said "Vouchered Request for Payment, Services Rendered."

"I'll fill out the most of it," Alex told me. "All you got to do is sign it."

"Uh huh. You, uh, got a pencil or something?"

"In the office. Just a second, I'll be right back."

Alex shuffled away again and I looked real quick to see what it was I was signing. And where. I'd never *heard* of such a thing as this form, much less seen one. But I was sure the real Riley Tanner was familiar enough with them.

Hmmmpf! How the heck about that. What the printing assured "vendors of goods and services" was that the United States government would stand good for the price of whatever they did for an "authorized agent" as indicated below.

What a jim-dandy idea this was.

Alex came back with a pencil and I quick as could be scrawled my signature. Okay, I wrote out Riley B. Tanner there instead of putting down my real name, which not only would've confused folks here in Broad Valley, but would have thoroughly baffled whatever clerk eventually had to make out a payment.

I felt kind of important when I signed that official document. After all, a person has to really be somebody before others will take his signature as payment for authorized goods and services, right? So yeah, I felt kind of puffed up and dignified when I signed that paper for Alex.

"And don't you worry, Marshal. I'll take good care of your horses. You want me to saddle one for you now or anything?"

"No," I told him, "I just wanted to see how things stand. You're doing a fine job here. I'm pleased an' want you to know it."

Alex looked a mite puffed up too when I told him that. We grinned at one another and shook hands, and I felt good about ugly being here when I turned to walk back to the Goodson house. Walked slow, though, and had to stop to rest a couple times along the way for I was getting awful tired by that time and was plenty grateful to be home when I got there.

THIRTY-EIGHT

Home. Lordy, I can't believe that word came into my mind. Home. Like hell. I hadn't had a home since a long time before I'd lit out from the place where I grew up. Not a real home, I hadn't.

And the Goodson place wasn't home to me neither, dammit. No place was, and that was a thing I needed to keep in mind. I had no home and wasn't fixing to. And if I did decide someday to find a place to light and put down roots, it wouldn't be some little patch of dusty nothing like Broad Valley, Texas, where people I didn't even know wanted to shoot me down for being somebody that I wasn't.

Lordy. I mean, that was really stupid. You know? Home. I knew better.

I was feeling pretty mad at myself when I got there. I marched around behind the church to the house and stomped up onto the porch. I don't know where Mrs. Goodson was, but Sarah heard me come in. She stepped to the kitchen door, a dish towel in her hand and a smile on her pretty face.

"We missed you for lunch, Marshal. Are you hungry? I could make up a plate of leftovers for you cold. Or if you like, I could heat something for you. Would you like . . . ?"

I didn't answer her. Pretended I didn't hear and went

scowling to the bedroom her and her folks had given to me
as if it was my own to use. Left Sarah standing in the
doorway there and stormed right away from her.

It was rude and unnecessary and cruel. But then I can be
a real dumb son of a bitch sometimes, excuse the language
please. Dumb and nasty and hurtful. And I knew that even
while I was in the middle of doing it.

I got inside that bedroom and wanted to slam the door
behind me, but that just would've made everything worse
so I settled for throwing my coat on the floor and kicking
my boots off and laying down on the bed rigid as a log
and feeling hateful toward the world and sorry for myself
all at the same damn time.

And the really stupid thing is that I was feeling all this
but didn't have the least idea why.

THIRTY-NINE

"Reverend Goodson . . ."
   "Call me Carl."

"Yes, sir, Re . . ." I shrugged and grinned at him. I just couldn't do it. He was a preacher, and I'd been taught that was something pretty special. You don't just go around calling preachers by their first names.

The Reverend Barber Goodson let me off the hook. He laughed and shrugged too, and I resolved that if I couldn't call him by his first name—and I couldn't—then at the least I'd try and not call him by anything at all as much as I could help it.

"Yes, sir," I said, trying again, "what I got to thinking was that, you being the town barber and everything, you prob'ly hear an awful lot. I mean, you know, from fellows sitting in your chair for a trim or a shave. Most fellas talk a little, don't they?"

"Oh, I wouldn't say they all do, of course. But most. Yes, I think it is safe to say that most men like to visit when they are in my chair."

"Yes, sir. So what I got to thinking was that maybe you've heard something that might could help me find out who tried to kill me, who it was that went and shot me in the back that day."

The Reverend Barber Goodson pursed his lips and steepled his fingertips beneath his chin. He stayed like that for a few seconds before he said anything. "I want to help you, of course. I hope you understand that."

"Yes, sir, I surely do. You and your family have more than helped, you've saved my life. I know you want to help me." I smiled. "Something else I know is that when a man starts a sentence with a claim that he 'wants to' do something, then it's real likely that the rest of what he says will be an explanation for why he can't."

The Reverend Barber Goodson laughed again. "You do know human nature, don't you? But then who better than an officer of the law to understand people."

Naturally I didn't correct him about that.

"You are quite right," he went on, "that although I 'want to' help you, I must be very careful about anything I say. As a barber I hear many things, of course. But as a man of the cloth, I hear even more. And anything I am told in my capacity as a minister, as a shepherd of the flock, must be kept completely confidential. Do you understand that, Marshal?"

"Yes, sir, I expect that I do. But what I'm asking about isn't a confession like, you know, like the Catholics do. D'you have confession in your church, Rev . . . I mean, uh, do you hear confessions like that too?"

"Not in the same way, of course, but a preacher is told certain things, Marshal, and those matters have to be, must be, held in confidence."

"Yes, sir. Well, like I was saying, what I'm asking about isn't what you might've heard in church but what you might've heard in your barbershop."

The Reverend Barber Goodson frowned and peered inside the tiny church he'd fashioned with his steepled fingers. He stayed that way for a little bit, and I didn't interrupt. "You raise an interesting point of ethics, Marshal."

"I do?"

"Unfortunately yes. You do."

"How's that, sir?"

"It is perfectly true that as a barber I could be expected to overhear many conversations and be told many things.

But it is also possible that, because I am also a pastor, I might well be told some things with the unspoken assumption that I would regard them as confidential. Even while the speaker happens to be seated in my barber's chair. He would still know me as his pastor, do you see? He might regard our conversation as being privileged by the cloth despite the physical circumstances of the moment. Am I making myself clear? A priest, for instance, would hold inviolate any confession made in the confessional booth, of course, but he would also be expected to remain silent about a confession made during a stroll down the street. Right?"

I grunted, not really sure what I'd think about that one until I had some time to do the thinking. But at first blush I'd say that it kinda made sense.

"And I believe the same might well apply to me, do you see. Anything told to me inside the church sanctuary would certainly be confidential. But shouldn't that apply as well to anything said to me in my shop, simply because the person who spoke knew me as a pastor as well as his barber?"

"I'm not for sure about that," I admitted.

The Reverend Barber Goodson sighed. "I am not positive about it either, to tell you the truth. But if I am going to err I would rather it be on the side of prudence. I'm sorry, Marshal, but that is the best I've been able to conclude so far."

"Are you telling me that you've been thinking about this before just this minute?" I asked.

He nodded.

"Which means you did hear something and you've been wondering your own self should you say anything about it to me."

"That isn't what I said."

"No, sir, but that's what it means."

He didn't answer me. Not that I expected him to.

"I won't ask you to do anything that you feel is wrong, sir. But can I ask you something else?"

"Of course. Anything."

"If you saw somebody point a gun at somebody else, would you holler for the person to duck?"

The Reverend Barber Goodson looked a mite offended. "Of course I would."

"But afterward, if that person went ahead and shot the other, you wouldn't say anything about it?"

"If I witnessed a crime, Marshal, it would certainly be my Christian duty to report completely and honestly on what I had seen. That would be right and proper. But if this hypothetical incident that you describe took place outside of my own personal knowledge and the person who did the shooting came to me in my role as his pastor and asked how he should go about seeking the Lord's forgiveness . . . that I would not relate to any living soul, Marshal. That I would not do."

"Is that sorta what's happened here, sir?"

He didn't answer. Not that I'd really expected he would. I thanked him and stood, my knee joints crackling. We'd been sitting on the front porch of the Goodson house, watching the night come and letting a fine dinner digest in our bellies.

"Time to turn in," I said. "If you'll excuse me, sir?"

"Marshal."

"Yes?"

"I want you to know that things are not as . . . cut and dried as your hypothetical example would present. I don't actually know, uh, any actual facts that would be valuable to you. I may be able to surmise some things. But it would only be guesswork really. I'm sorry."

"Yes, sir. Can I ask you something else?"

"Of course."

"That word you used. Hypno . . . What was it again?"

"Hypothetical?"

"That's the one. It means . . . ?"

"A supposition, Marshal. A hypothetical question is one that describes a what-if situation and not necessarily an actual one."

"Yes, sir. That's kind of what I thought. Thank you, Reverend."

He opened his mouth as if to correct me and I'm sure he wanted again to invite me to call him by first name, but he didn't bother saying it again. Instead he smiled a little and settled for wishing me a good night.

FORTY

Nobody knew. Nobody saw. Nobody suspected. Nobody guessed. Wherever I went and whoever I asked, the answers were always the same. Nope, sorry, don't know nothing about who might've shot at you. Wasn't me. Sorry. Wish I could help, but I can't.

I couldn't say that I was surprised by any of this, of course. Even innocent men don't like to say much to John Law.

Or so I've been informed. I can't say for certain sure that I've ever actually met an innocent man to prove this theory on, so I can't exactly swear to that, but it is what I'm given to understand.

For sure I've been questioned plenty enough times my own self and never volunteered anything to the law, not even when the guy they were after happened to be somebody I had a grudge against. No, it's never been my policy to give anything or anyone up to the dang law.

Heck, I recall one time out in Colorado I was having a quiet, peaceful evening meal when a half dozen fellows rode up on me, every one of them sporting a shiny badge on his chest and a big gun on his belt.

They were after some jasper who'd held up a whiskey drummer across the border in Kansas. What they were doing chasing the robber across a boundary like that I didn't know and didn't ask. Maybe the salesman was kin or something like that to set them off so determined.

Anyway, they came on me unexpected, but what could I do except be hospitable, it being that time of evening and my coffeepot having started to smell almighty good by then. I invited them to step down and join me for however long my coffee and beans held out, and they did.

They staked their horses out and had some coffee. Then one of them went down to the creek to bring more water while another pounded some coffee beans so we could make a second pot and satisfy everybody's thirst. They had some bacon with them that they added to my beans, and one fellow brought out some canned pears. I would say that we had a fine meal by the time we were all done, and after a while I assured them that I hadn't seen the least hair on this dastard they were chasing.

After we'd all eaten and had some palaver, this posse—I still remember that Kansas sheriffs name too, Johnny Mueller he was—thanked me. The one with the pears noted how I'd enjoyed them and left a spare can for my breakfast come morning.

I offered to let them stay the night at my fire, but they said no, said they needed to be getting on about the business of finding the whiskey salesman's robber. We shook hands and parted friends.

I would have to admit, though, that my hospitality that evening wasn't all it might have been. I neglected to share the bottles of whiskey I had in my saddlebags at the time.

But then you see, I didn't recall if there was anything written on the labels of those bottles that might identify them as a salesman's samples.

Anyhow, it wasn't entirely a surprise for me now to discover that the good folk of Broad Valley, Texas, weren't any more forthcoming about answering questions from the law than I'd always been myself.

I did try, though. Walked that town one end to the other and spoke to just about everybody I could get within earshot of. Didn't learn a darn thing, but I did get some exercise and was pleased to learn that the more time went by the better and more spry I was feeling. My recovery from the gunshot was coming right along, and the truth was that I could've crawled on top of ugly and moved myself along any day I wanted at that point.

But the rest of the truth was that I was tired of moving along. Tired of running.

I'd run from the law practically my whole life long and never thought a bad thing about that. Always considered it a pretty sensible habit for a gentleman in my particular line of work, in fact.

This time, though, I was the one who was the law. Kinda. And I was finding that I was feeling offended, both personally and professionally, to've been shot down from ambush like that.

It would please me no end to find out who'd done that and have some serious words with him on the subject.

So even though I could've ridden right on out of there and got on my way south again the way I'd first intended, I stayed put there in Broad Valley.

Which only goes to prove that I can be kinda dumb sometimes.

FORTY-ONE

Now, the truth is that I wasn't much of a hand when the subject turned to murder. I mean, that just plain was not the line of work that I was in nor did I know all that much about it. I'm a thief. A darn good one if I do say so. But shooting folks for no good reason . . .

I was thinking along those lines, see, when it occurred to me that mayhap I was on to something right there with that simple thought: Shooting folks with no good reason.

Except when you get right down to it, *there is no such thing*. Ever.

Whoever it was that shot at me, he had a reason. A good and entirely logical reason, at least to his mind. That is just the way things are. Never mind what sort of thing you are talking about, a fellow never does anything that he doesn't think is justified.

There are whole lots of people who think that taking money from somebody else is wrong. Well, in a manner of speaking, and certainly in the view of the law, it may be wrong. But you see, there's wrong and then again there's . . . uh . . . less wrong, shall we say.

Committing a holdup, now that is certainly against the law. But just how wrong it is kinda depends on which side of the pistol you happen to be standing.

I prefer to rob banks, stagecoaches, like that. Really what

it is, I prefer to take money from companies instead of from folks. And those companies, banks and express lines and the like, are indemnified—didn't think I'd know a word like that, huh—they're covered by insurance. So it isn't even their own money that I'm taking but some back-east insurance outfit.

As for the occasional fellow that I might stick up, well, I wouldn't do that unless I knew for certain sure that the guy was rich and could afford it. I mean, I wouldn't stoop to stealing milk money from a starving widow or anything like that. I have my standards. I have my pride.

And I've never once known any other outlaw who didn't think he was right to do what he done. What he did, I mean. Point is, everybody feels justified to do what it is that he's doing. Guaranteed. That is basic human nature.

Don't believe me? I spent a night in a jail cell in Skiatook once. That's up in the Nations. Creek country? Cherokee? One of those, I can't remember for sure which tribe. Anyhow, I slept off a celebration there once and woke up in a cell that was crowded full of gents I remembered partying with the night before. The cell next to this one was occupied by one lone fellow. Scrawny little runt-of-the-litter sort of man with a scraggly mustache and rheumy eyes and teeth so brown I thought he didn't have any until the light got strong and I could see them better.

I was the first one of the party crowd to wake up, and this fellow on the other side of the bars from me was awake too, and naturally I got to complaining about being shoved into that crowded cell that stunk of vomit and passed wind and other smells that I'd rather not even think where they came from. But there I was, packed in with those other fellas like pigs in a sty, and there this ugly little fellow sat with a cell all to himself.

I said something about that and the little guy commenced to grin and act proud of himself.

He was in there alone, he allowed, because he was too dangerous an hombre to be trusted in arm's reach of anyone else.

Now, I got to tell you, I was sitting side by side with him, with just a stand of iron bars separating us, and after looking this little guy up and down a few times I did not feel like I needed to move away to where he couldn't reach me.

Naturally enough after an introduction like that I asked the man what he was in for and why he should be considered so dangerous.

He sounded downright proud of himself when he explained it. He was in there for murder. Several murders, in fact. And I didn't even have to prompt him to get the full of the story about it.

Seems he'd killed two of Skiatook's soiled doves and dang near killed the other three in the town's one and only house of late night relaxation. And while he was about it, he came near to killing two of the local gentry who'd been customers at the time.

Now, I could just imagine how a thing like that would peeve the townsfolk. Murder apart, this little guy had rendered Skiatook virtually free of prostitution in one swell foop. So naturally enough I asked him why he'd gone and done a thing like that.

It seems he'd killed two people and came near to killing five more because they insulted him. Well, not all of them insulted him. Exactly. But the old bawd who ran the place sure insulted him, and the others were no better than she was, so they every one deserved what they got.

He was real clear about that. Had no more remorse than a buzzard would have sympathy for a dead jackrabbit lying on the prairie. They every one deserved what-all they got.

Heck, he sounded real proud of himself. Even bragged that he'd done it the hard way, without a gun. Although he was an honest enough man to admit that he would of used a gun if he'd owned one. Since he didn't, and since he felt entirely justified to teach those people a lesson, he went in with a chunk of firewood that he picked up off the woodpile and began laying about with it. Busted the skulls of several of the women and one of the men before anybody much realized what was going on, and even then it took half a dozen or more to wrestle him down and get the club away from him.

I couldn't help myself. I had to ask what it was the madam there had done that was so insulting, and he puffed up like a rooster puffing its feathers. "She told me she wouldn't let me have one of her girls 'less I went and took a bath first. Can you imagine that? And her all caked with powder so old it looked gray so I knew she hadn't had a bath herself since the past winter prob'ly. Can you imagine?"

Yeah, that sounded like reason enough to kill some people over, I thought to myself. Sure it did, I thought as I moved a little further away from the bars that divided his cell from mine.

But you see, it really and truly did justify the whole thing so far as this little runt saw things.

Which, of course, is my point about all this.

A man does things for a reason.

And generally speaking, once I got to thinking on the subject, there just aren't all that many reasons why a fellow might go and take a shot at somebody else. Revenge. Pride. Jealousy. That good old standby Money. Take your pick.

So what occurred to me now was that if I was having trouble finding out who, maybe I should starting looking for reasons why.

And that in turn might could lead to some ideas about who.

I felt somewhat better after coming to that resolution.

Oh, the little fellow in Skiatook? They hanged him, of course. But I hear that he said right to the end that those sons of bitches had it coming to them every one, the madam for insulting him and the customers for taking her side in the fuss. He didn't regret a single lick he'd gotten in against them.

Just like no doubt the man that shot me felt he was justified in doing it, whether that was from fear, for money, whatever.

I pondered that late into the night while I lay awake in my borrowed bed in the Goodson home with Sarah so near I could practically breathe in the scent of her hair and so . . . ah, never mind. Best I put that sort of thought out of mind, her being a decent girl and me being, well, not exactly what she thought me to be.

Still and all, it was a long time before I got to sleep that night.

FORTY-TWO

Now, the fact was that I was under a rare disadvantage here. Seeing as I'd only been Deputy Marshal Riley B. Tanner for a matter of weeks, I had no way to know who-all the good marshal might already know here in Broad Valley. Or who he was after and therefore who-all it was that would have cause to be afraid of Tanner's presence. Or who he might have offended in the past. Whose kin he could have arrested or even killed in the line of duty.

I mean, there was no end to the number of grudges, fears and what-not that might could lie between the dead marshal and somebody in this town.

And of course the other party, whoever he was and for whatever reason he wanted Tanner dead, had no way to know that I didn't possess Riley Tanner's knowledge of past deeds.

Nor, darn it, did I want anybody to know.

I didn't have such an unsullied past my own self that I could count on convincing a jury of my innocence if it came out that the real marshal was dead but that I denied having anything to do with getting him into that condition.

No, I was the only one who knew what really happened to Tanner or where the body was. And I dang sure wanted to keep it that way.

So I guessed about the best thing I could do was to put

my thinking cap on and do some serious detecting.

Huh. I sure could've used some of a marshal's know-how to help me along.

Not having that, of course, I was just going to have to muddle along the best I knew how.

"More coffee, Marshal?"

"Thank you, Miss Goodson. I'd like that."

Lordy, but this was one pretty girl. She jumped up with a smile and came all the way around to the other side of the table to fetch the big pot off the stove, then carried it over and filled my cup for me, smiling all the while.

She leaned down close when she poured the coffee, and my field of vision was full to overflowing with . . . um . . . light blue gingham check cloth and never mind what that cloth was filled with. I think I started to sweat a little even though the house still held the morning cool in it.

Heck, I was a guest in this house. And a fellow with a position to uphold, so to speak, never mind that the dignity of it wasn't exactly mine but only borrowed.

For sure I shouldn't ought to be thinking the things that I found myself thinking. Not with Sarah Goodson being a decent girl, danggit.

It's one thing to make one's thoughts free with the likes of loose women and amateur tarts. But it would be a shameful thing to abuse the hospitality of folks as fine as the Goodson family. I just couldn't bring myself to do that.

But then I shouldn't allow myself to think so much as I was about the Goodsons' daughter either.

The girl poured my cup full, and she was so near that now I really could breathe her scent. She smelled of soap and some delicate, sweet, flowery scent too. Some sort of cologne maybe? It sure wasn't anything I'd ever come across in a barbershop, but then it's not a subject that I know anything about. The one thing I was sure of was that Sarah Goodson smelt almighty fine and it wouldn't have angered me if she'd stood there for, say, the next hour or two so I could smell of her and, uh, continue to admire the cut of that gingham dress.

Unfortunately it didn't take her real long to pour a cup of coffee. Darn it. She finished the task and stepped back half a pace and gave me a huge, sweet, innocent smile.

I managed to keep from groaning out loud, and I am proud of myself for being able to hold it in like I did. It wasn't easy.

"Tha'ns," I croaked, mangling even that simple little word. But at least I was able to get some sound out of my throat. That was a wonder since it felt tight and all packed full. I felt some heat coming into my cheeks and faked a cough so as to give me an excuse to put a hand over my face.

"Thanks," I said, more clearly this time, once I had things under control again.

Sarah's smile bloomed once more and she touched my wrist before she turned away to take the coffeepot back to the range.

I noticed that the wood box was running low and realized that now I was feeling better I should start trying to be helpful around the place. I could take over things like bringing in wood and keeping the water reservoir filled. Stuff like that.

But that was not a matter of wanting to curry favor with Sarah, I told myself in no uncertain terms. No sir, it was not. I was only wanting to be a good guest in the house, that was all.

Uh huh. I had a sip of the coffee Sarah'd poured. Sure tasted good to me.

FORTY-THREE

"Rev . . . Mist . . . uh, sir?" I just couldn't bring myself to call the man by his first name. Couldn't make my tongue fit around it no matter how hard I tried. The Reverend Barber Goodson smiled at my dilemma and patiently waited for me to spit the question out. "I know you need to get the shop open, but could I walk along with you, please? There's some things I'd like to know."

"As long as they are things I am free to tell you, of course I'll be glad to help." He smiled again. "Be glad for the company too for that matter. Come along if you like." He reached down his coat off the peg beside the front door, and I pulled on a vest. It wasn't all that cold of late. I also took down the gunbelt I'd taken to hanging there. None of the family had ever said a word about me bringing a gun into their home, but I hadn't wanted to maybe offend by wearing it indoors with them.

"A pity you feel that you need that," the reverend observed as I strapped the belt on and made sure everything hung snug and comfortable and where it was supposed to be. A gun isn't something you want to have to go searching for in times of need. You want to know right where that thing is to begin with.

"Yes, sir," I said, "but I expect it's just like with any

other workman's tools. The important thing is what you do with them, right?''

"I hadn't thought of it in quite that way, but yes. That would indeed be right, wouldn't it.''

We went outside and down the porch steps, walked past the church and out onto the road. It amazed me how ordinary Broad Valley was to me now. It's a funny thing. You come up to something new—a town, a mountain . . . a person—and you really pay attention to them. You really *see* them, if you know what I mean. But after that, once the new is worn off and you're used to what you're seeing, after that you just accept them as ordinary and don't really see them ever again in quite that same brand-new way.

It was like that now with Broad Valley. It looked humdrum and normal to me and I didn't even have to think about how to get from the church into town and on to Goodson's barbershop.

We strolled along and I asked my host about stuff like the local politics—it's been my experience that some people can get pretty riled and nasty when it comes to political divisions—but he said there wasn't anything exciting happening in that regard. They'd had a quiet election the previous fall, and most of the local officials, town and county alike, had four years to go before they'd face the voters again. So I ruled that out as a likely cause behind somebody wanting to murder a deputy U.S. marshal.

"Any feuds hereabout?" I asked.

Goodson shook his head. "No, none. And that is something I would certainly know about if there were any.'' He smiled a very small smile. "It would amaze you the things people bring to their pastor. I think I can say with good authority that there are no feuds ongoing.''

I mentally crossed that possibility off my list too.

"Unsolved crimes?'' I asked.

"Nothing of any consequence. Of course Sheriff Frake could give you much better information than I can. But I know of nothing serious.''

"No big robberies with the money unrecovered? No murders or, um, assaults on ladies? Nothing like that?''

He shook his head. "This is a law-abiding community.

Well, apart from someone trying to murder you, that is.'' The Reverend Goodson didn't seem to see anything funny in his statement. I did.

"Good folks here," I said.

"Yes, very."

"No problems."

"Not usually."

"Is there anything at all unusual that's been happening? Anything you can think of and never mind d'you think it could relate to my problems."

He took a second to think that one over before he answered, and his gait slowed just a little as he pondered. After a few seconds he speeded up again and shrugged. "The only thing at all out of the ordinary is a slight loss of population."

"Folks dying?" I asked.

"Oh, nothing so dramatic. A run of bad luck, I suppose you would say. Families losing their land and moving on. Not many, understand. I probably wouldn't even be aware of it except that I can see the decrease in my congregation on Sundays. And a few have dropped by asking for counsel and prayer. It has been sad, let me tell you."

"I'm sure. What's done it? Drought? Pests? That sort of thing?"

Goodson's brow knitted. We reached his shop, and he dug into a pocket for his keys. "No, and that is an odd thing, isn't it. Our weather has been normal enough. Certainly there have been no shortages of rainfall or exceptional cold. Nor heat for that matter. No, everything really has been quite normal."

"So what's been driving them away?"

"Poor business practices? I suppose you would have to put it that way."

"All of them?"

"I guess . . . I hadn't really thought of these failures as parts of a whole, you understand. Hadn't thought of them all together before now but as individual, isolated instances. But . . . now that you ask . . . yes, I believe. Pretty much all of them."

"All farmers?" I asked.

"No. Mostly it was farms that failed, but there were several ranchers with small holdings who also went under."

"Foolish men, were they? Or green to what they were
doing?"

"Not particularly, I . . . *No!!!*"

Goodson screamed, his eyes bugging wide at the sight
of something behind me, and before I hardly had time to
react he gave me a shove that sent me tottering off the
sidewalk and out into the street.

The same time as he was doing that there was the loud
bark of a gunshot and the wet, ugly thump of a bullet finding meat. Carl Goodson grunted and dropped to his knees.

I staggered, trying to get my balance. My Colt was already in hand, though I don't remember taking time to think
about grabbing it.

A rod or so distant, there at the street corner, a man I
was sure I'd never seen before stood with a pistol in hand
and smoke still drifting from its muzzle.

I fired. Put a bullet into his chest, and he sagged at the
knees. I fired again and knew I'd hit him a second time
somewhere in the upper body.

The man looked at me. Tried to take aim in my direction,
so I shot him a third time. This time in the face. He went
down. Permanent, I was sure.

The hell with him, though.

I darted back up onto the sidewalk to where Carl Goodson lay with blood spreading out into a pool underneath
him.

FORTY-FOUR

I didn't know there were that many people who lived in the town. Nor for a dozen miles around, for that matter. It was like somebody announced it from the rooftops that Rev. Carl Goodson had been shot, and everybody who heard came running to help.

The bad thing—aside from the fact of him being shot in the first place—was that Goodson himself was as close as Broad Valley came to having a doctor.

The good thing is that he wasn't wounded all that serious.

The assassin's bullet entered just above his belt on his left side and raked through his body passing not deeper than an inch or two beneath the skin before exiting around toward his back. We pulled his clothing open first thing, of course, and the wound was an ugly, awful-looking thing, purple and bloodshot and leaking, but I was pretty sure the bullet never went deep enough to damage any organs or anything like that. I figured so long as the openings didn't turn rotten he should recover quick enough.

Somebody brought a door to carry him on and somebody else ran and got Mrs. Goodson and Sarah from the house. A bunch of us started off carrying him toward the house, but Mrs. Goodson met us partway there and said no, she wanted him taken back to the barbershop, where he had his

medicines and implements and things, so we turned around
and toted him back the way we'd just come.

We laid the door with Goodson on it across some chairs,
and Mrs. Goodson picked through a bag of strange-looking
tools to find what-all she wanted. She seemed to know what
she was doing, and everybody left her alone about it. For
sure I wouldn't have known to contradict her about anything.

"Jim, run down the street to Maxwell's and get me a
ladies' scarf. A silk one. Quick now."

A man I didn't know bobbed his head and ran out the
door. Which was something of a feat for the place was
filling up so tight it would soon be difficult finding room
enough to draw a deep breath. About half the town was
crowding inside.

It occurred to me that I was supposed to have some authority, so I set about shooing people outside while Mrs.
Goodson did things that I didn't really want to watch anyway.

I know, because I peeked when I shouldn't have. Once
Mrs. Goodson had the silk scarf she'd wanted, she doused
the thing with some liquid, fastened one corner of it to a
long skinny rod and then pushed the whole dang affair
clean through her husband's wound.

He'd been lying there pale and panting on the door, but
when she did that he screamed once and passed out. Which
was probably for the better anyhow.

"That should take care of any sepsis, please God," she
said when the now bloody scarf was pulled all the way
through. "Hand me that gauze, will you?"

Somebody passed her a wad of white cloth, and she used
that to make bandage pads over the wound where the bullet
had gone in and the one where it'd come back out again.
At least she hadn't had to probe around inside him for a
bullet lodged there. That can be unpleasant.

"Blankets. Does anyone have any blankets?" she asked.

No one did, but a number of coats got donated quick and
were piled over top of the unconscious man.

"We can carry him back to the house now if you would
please, gentlemen," Mrs. Goodson said.

There were more than enough hands eager to help, so this time I hung back. Mrs. Goodson had it all under control so far as Carl was concerned—funny how I was thinking of him by name now that he was wounded—and there were other things that I wanted to look into.

The men swarmed around and lifted up Carl Goodson, still lying on that door, like a swarm of ants intent on dragging a dead beetle home. They picked him up and bore him away, and I let them all go on.

When the last of them was gone, I stepped outside and kicked around in the dirt beside the sidewalk until I found the ring of keys Carl had dropped when he was shot. I went back inside to blow out the lamps that'd been lighted while Mrs. Goodson was tending to her husband's wounds—the family had enough grief on my account; they didn't need a fire to destroy their livelihood on top of everything else—then closed the shop tight and locked the door behind me.

Somebody—I didn't know who or when—had already carried the body of the would-be murderer away.

I went off to find it.

FORTY-FIVE

For lack of any better idea, I suppose, the body was laid out in an otherwise vacant cell at the sheriff's office. Herb Frake was there in the office. He seemed pleased to see me.

"What happened this morning?" he asked. "Did Phylo try to murder the reverend?"

"Not exactly." I explained the way it had been for him while the sheriff sat there nodding and chewing the inside of his cheek and jotting down the occasional note about what I was saying.

"Justifiable, of course," he grunted when I was done. "I'll take it before a coroner's inquest eventually," he said, "but unless you can think of some reason why we should be in a big hurry about this I won't bother convening a jury until the next regular circuit court session. No sense in adding to the county's expenses. Is that all right with you, Marshal?"

I had about forgotten that I was supposed to know all about this stuff. Which I didn't. Heck, I barely understood what the man was talking about, but didn't want to lay my ignorance out there for everyone to admire. Naturally I told him that whatever he wanted was just fine by me. And that was the truth. Sheriff Frake didn't know the half of how fine it was by me.

"Phylo," I said then. "Is that the man I shot?"

Frake nodded. "Phylo Barnes. Do you want to see him?"

"I expect I should."

The sheriff took me into the cell where this Barnes fellow's body was laid out—on the bare boards of the bunk; the mattress ticking and blanket had been taken off so as to keep them from getting blood on them—and said, "There he is, for whatever good it will do you."

The sheriff sounded as if he didn't much like looking at the mess my last bullet had made of Barnes's head. Well, I couldn't say that I liked it all that much either. But better him than me. Or Carl Goodson, for that matter.

"What can you tell me about him?" I asked.

"He's a cowhand. Or was, I should say. He's ridden for three or four different outfits around here. I don't know where he's from or if he has kin anywhere that we should notify. I'll have to ask about that. Someone out at the Rocker M might know. He rode for them longer than anyone else, I think, and the most recent."

"Rocker M?"

"They're north of town. The biggest outfit in this part of the country."

"And Barnes worked there?"

Frake nodded. "The last I heard, anyway."

"Was he a hothead? In trouble with the law much?"

"Not really. Oh, I knew him, all right. But no more so than most and a lot less trouble than some. I'd have him in here overnight for drunk and disorderly now and then. And once he beat up another cowboy. Threatened to kill him. But it didn't come to anything. The two of them fought. Bloodied each other up a little. That's all. Barnes won, and the other fellow drew his time."

Frake stopped for a moment, then said, "You know, I hadn't ever particularly given it any thought before, but after that other fellow drew his time . . . Wigman? Whigham? something like that, his name was . . . after he drew his pay and signed off the Rocker M he wasn't ever seen around here again. I never thought that much of it at the time. Cowboys come and go like fleas on a dog's back.

There's no keeping track of them. But now that I think about it, I wonder if Phylo here could have continued his feud with that Wiggin . . . that was it, by damn, Dan Wiggin . . . I wonder if Barnes waited for his chance and murdered Wiggin for his pay.''

"Too late t'ask now," I said.

"We know for sure he was willing enough to murder you."

"Would have done it sure if it hadn't been for Carl Goodson. That's twice I owe that man my life."

"You were lucky."

"Don't I just know it." I stepped further into the cell and stood for a moment beside the body of the man I'd just killed.

I would have thought I'd feel something, doing that. I mean, this had been a human person, and I'd taken his life. Shot him down and killed him. Oh, it was self-defense, no doubt about that. But still and all, he'd been alive this morning and now he was dead—ugly dead with his head all busted open and misshapen like it was—and it was by my hand that he got that way.

Yet I felt . . . not all that much really. It was something that'd had to be done, and I'd done it, and now it was over. The only real regret I had was that Carl was laying there hurting because of this cowboy. Because this dead man here tried to kill me and failed.

So I expected to feel something deep and meaningful but all I was feeling was anger. Anger that this SOB had tried to kill me and anger that he'd shot Carl.

Anger and curiosity too, actually.

Why had a complete stranger like this gone and tried to shoot me down in the street?

Two, three times, maybe? Had this Phylo Barnes been the same one that tried to kill me before?

Those times hadn't made any better sense to me than this one did.

I thought about that sort of thing for a little while. Then I stepped forward and bent down to the dead man.

It felt funny to touch him. I mean, he was dead. He wasn't going to get ticklish and try to scooch away from me. His head was split open like a melon dropped on hard ground, and one look at him proved he was as dead as dead ever gets. So it wasn't that. But I felt a little odd doing what I had to do.

Made myself do it, though, as it needed done. I bent down and started going through the dead man's pockets.

Now, *that* made me feel more squeamish than anything else about this.

But this wasn't robbery, and Phylo Barnes wasn't just some ordinary dead guy. This was a dead guy who'd tried to make me dead, so I figured the circumstances were what you would call extenuating.

"Let's see what your Mr. Barnes has on him, shall we, Sheriff?" I said in as light and breezy a tone as I could manage.

FORTY-SIX

"Tell me something, Sheriff? Does the Rocker M pay so good that a cowhand like this Barnes would have forty dollars in gold in his pocket on the . . . ," I looked at the calendar on the sheriff's office wall, ". . . the fourteenth day of the month?"

"This is the sixteenth."

"Is it? Sorry. All right then. Should a man like Barnes have four eagles in his pocket this far from payday?"

"Not on the best day of his life," Sheriff Frake agreed. "Especially since a regular hand like Barnes would only draw thirty for the month."

I wasn't exactly surprised. I looked down at the contents of Barnes's pockets, which we'd laid out on top of the sheriff's desk. It wasn't all that much of a legacy for a man to leave behind him. There were the four gleaming, ten-dollar eagle coins plus an assortment of small pocket change totaling $1.14. There was a Barlow knife with a blade made thin from being sharpened for years and years. A small key that might have fit most anything. A blue bandanna. And that was it save for a wisp of balled-up thread that I hadn't thought was there on purpose but was just left over from the last time his pants were washed.

Those few items. Oh yes. He'd also had his gun. I looked at that too, of course. Sheriff Frake had it tucked away in a drawer. For evidence, I supposed, when he finally got around to going to the coroner's jury. Phylo Barnes's pistol was a Smith and Wesson .44. It showed wear from being carried but was clean enough. Fresh cleaned, probably. I would think a man would want to clean his gun before he set out to commit a murder from ambush. The cylinder was chambered for six cartridges but Barnes had loaded only four—one of those now spent when he shot Carl. The cartridge loops in his gunbelt were every one of them empty.

Now, I admit that I don't know a heckuva heap when it comes to detecting and investigating and all that. But I'm not entirely stupid. And common sense told me that if I had more than forty dollars in my kick and was setting out to commit murder, I'd at the very least want to stop and buy me enough cartridges to fill up the cylinder of my gun.

Unless I'd just real extra recent come into possession of both the money and the desire to shoot somebody?

Made sense when I thought about it.

This Phylo Barnes fellow more than likely was hired to kill me. Danged if I could figure out why, or by who, but I kinda had to come to the conclusion that that was what happened. I told Sheriff Frake so.

"That sounds reasonable to me. You, uh, have no idea who might be behind this, you say?"

"No, sir, I surely don't." And wasn't *that* the natural truth. Of course I didn't go into detail with the sheriff about why and how I would explain that. I didn't want to confuse him with side issues to be thinking about.

"Someone out at the Rocker M, do you think?" Frake suggested.

"It's a place to start looking anyway, isn't it," I agreed.

"I tell you what, Marshal. Why don't you ask at the Rocker M. While you're doing that, I'll check around in town to see if anyone remembers Phylo being here last night. If he was seen talking to someone, that might give us a lead on where else to make inquiries."

"All right, and I thank you." I figured the local folks would be a lot more comfortable talking to a man they knew, like Sheriff Frake, than they would with a stranger like me.

Something else occurred to me and I sighed some and shook my head.

"What is it?"

"I was just thinking, looking at those coins laying there. Forty bucks. A man likes to think his life should be worth more'n that."

Frake smiled. "If it makes you feel any better, Marshal, remember that for a job like murder the normal style would be for the head man to make a down payment on the job. There's no telling how much more Barnes expected to collect after he'd completed his work."

"You surely do know how to make a boy feel better, Sheriff."

Frake laughed.

"Would you mind giving me directions to the Rocker M? I expect I'll ride out there and talk to some folks. Who knows. Maybe it'll even do some good."

FORTY-SEVEN

It felt good to be up on old ugly again. It'd been weeks, and the miserable cayuse was frisky when I first stepped onto him. I had to remind him which of us was in charge. Then we headed north following the directions Sheriff Frake gave me. I bet I didn't take us more than two, three miles out of the proper way before I came over a small rise and saw the Rocker M headquarters sprawled in and around a stand of artificially planted trees.

They were real trees, of course, but their location was carefully planned so the leafy ones would offer shade and the skinny, evergreen ones would act as a windbreak. All very sensible, of course.

The house was big, ornate and painted. White. With dark green shutters. Very impressive, that.

There were also a number of outbuildings, some of them showing smoke. Barns, sheds, corrals and all the usual. It all looked tidy. And expensive. The owner had money. As I came closer I could see that he also seemed to've come here with lessons to be learned and that he was capable of learning them.

That's because one of the outbuildings was an obvious henhouse, set over close to what was just as obviously the remains of a garden patch. Very ordinary and sensible, right? You put your chicken house close to the garden so the hens can eat any bugs that might want to chew on your vegetables. You do things that way just about every place civilized.

Anyway, in a friendlier area what was originally built here would have been right and proper. But here you can't draw enough water to keep a garden. Not the way moisture evaporates into the hot, dry wind through what should be the summer growing season, you can't. Which I suspected was what would've done for the garden. As for the chickens, you can't civilize hawks and coyotes any easier than you can tame land. Can't shoot them all either, and it isn't only folks that like the taste of fresh chickens.

The Rocker M had tried to make a civilized place here, but they'd failed on those two counts anyway.

I rode into the yard and looked around. Generally speaking the polite thing is for a man to stay in the saddle until he's invited down. On the other hand there wasn't any bell or other way to announce my arrival. I sat atop ugly thinking about it for a minute and the problem resolved itself when a man with skin so shiny black it looked polished came to the front door and stepped out onto the porch. He was wearing an apron over his regular clothes. He also had a large-bore shotgun—single barrel but that didn't inspire me to any confidence—in his hands. He wasn't pointing it or acting threatening. Just kinda . . . holding it. Like he'd only happened to be carrying it when he saw or heard my coming.

"Something I can do for you, mister?"

"I'm looking for the boss," I told him.

"Foreman's out with the hands. You can find a meal at the cookhouse around the side there." He inclined his head to show me which side he meant. "If you're looking for a job, go ahead and eat, then wait there for the foreman. His name is Jenson. He'll be in around dark."

"Not him I'm looking for, but I thank you for the offer. Sheriff Frake told me this place is owned by a gentleman named Randall Moore. It's Mr. Moore I came to talk with."

"If you're looking for a job . . ."

"I'm Deputy Marshal Tanner," I announced, just as bold as brass. It sounded strange to me, claiming it right out like that, but I didn't see that I had much choice in the matter. "The visit is official."

"In that case, Marshal, step down if you like. I'll tell the colonel you're here."

Colonel, huh? The sheriff hadn't mentioned that to me. But then there likely was no reason why he should.

Especially since colonels, majors, captains, they were thick as lice in the cow business. I'd noticed that up home in Kansas. Half the Texans that came up the trails carried some military title or other, and the better dressed they were the bigger the rank they still wanted to be called.

Something else that I'd noticed was that as the years passed and the number of cows sold continued to fatten those fellows' bank accounts, the ranks got higher and higher. I personally knew—okay, knew *of*—one man from somewhere down this way who'd grown from a corporal to a lieutenant to a captain and lastly to a colonel. And all of this promotion coming after the dang war was over.

This so-called colonel then was likely another unrecon-structed Texas Confederate, I figured.

Not that it was any of my nevermind.

I crawled down off ugly and did a few squats to limber up my knees while the black man went inside to see the great man. There wasn't any place to tie ugly so I stood there holding the reins, and after a minute the black man came back out—no shotgun this time, which I took to be a good sign—and took ugly from me.

"Go on in, sir. The colonel's office is into the foyer and to the left. He's expecting you."

I thanked him and trotted up the steps to the cool shade of the porch and on inside.

FORTY-EIGHT

So maybe I'd misjudged this particular colonel. It didn't take any special powers of observation to see that the man who greeted me likely only missed becoming a general because of the wound that left him with only one arm. He had the sort of presence that just makes you know that he had authority. Nobody'd had to give him command. A man like this would take charge of things as natural as he took to breathing.

He held his left hand out to me—there wasn't but a stump where his right arm should have been, a fact which his tailor accommodated but didn't bother trying to hide—and welcomed me by name. All of my name. Which I hadn't completely given to the black man.

"You were expecting me, Colonel?" Funny, but the title sounded perfectly natural.

"Not specifically. I'd heard about your arrival, of course. And your wound. I'm glad you survived the ordeal. Wounds are a subject I happen to know something about."

"Yes, I see."

"Will you join me?" He pointed to a tray that had a silver pot on it and some cups.

"Yes, sir, I would." I expected him to call the black man in to pour, but he didn't. He managed it himself, not at all clumsy with only the one hand. But then he'd had plenty of time to practice.

"Milk? Sugar?"

"I'll just take it black, thank you."

He nodded and handed me the cup, then indicated a chair. I carried my cup there while Colonel Moore poured for himself, stirred some fixings in and sat in a wingback chair with the cup and saucer in his lap.

I had a sip of the liquid and discovered that it wasn't coffee but tea. I managed to keep from making a face and wondered if it was too late . . . the heck with it. "Mind if I change my mind about the milk and sugar?"

"Please."

I got up and went to repair the damage.

The colonel smiled. "I was wondering what sort of man you are, Marshal. You've just told me."

"How is that, sir?"

"You're polite but not afraid to admit to a mistake. I like that."

"Either that or I just can't abide tea without stuff in it," I told him and returned to my seat in a chair that matched his.

"Yes, whatever. May I ask what brings you here this afternoon?"

"I want to find out about one of your hands. Man name of Phylo Barnes."

"Former hand," Moore said.

"Pardon?"

"My foreman fired Barnes some days ago. He had been employed here in the past but no longer. This would have been, mm, four days ago? I believe so. Jenson warned him several times about being quarrelsome, but Barnes refused to mend his ways. Jenson chose to lay him off. He came here . . . yes, I'm sure it was four days ago. He came to me to collect his final wage."

"Do you recall how much that was?"

"Yes, I do. Eleven dollars. Exactly."

Which did not account for the forty in gold Barnes had on him when he died. "Paid exactly how, if you don't mind."

"One half eagle and six silver dollars. I assume there is a reason why you would ask a question like that?" the colonel said.

"Yes, sir." It occurred to me that he gave me the answer before he questioned why I might want to know. I told him what'd happened in town.

"I see."

"Can you think of any reason . . . ?"

"Sorry. None. Not that I am intimately familiar with the everyday thoughts of the hands. But no, I know of no reason why Barnes might have done such a thing. You're welcome to question my foreman or the other hands. One of them might know."

"They'll be back this evening?"

"Yes. You are welcome to stay for supper and to spend the night here if you like. Speak with anyone you wish. I see no reason why they would not cooperate. If you like I shall issue instructions for them to do so."

"That won't be necessary, sir."

I took a sip of the tea—I didn't much like the stuff still but it was sure better with the sugar than without—and glanced at the wall behind the colonel. I was surprised by what I saw there.

Among other things like mounted deer heads and framed certificates there were some fading tintypes. Daguerreotypes. Whatever the darn things are supposed to be called.

They showed bodies of uniformed men in mass, several of them with smaller groupings of people, a couple of individual soldiers. All but one, a very old one that showed a stiffly posed man and woman with a baby in their lap, were of the military. The baby was wearing a dress. I wondered if it was the colonel, although it was a little hard now to think of him as having been a wee infant.

The thing that surprised me though was that the uniforms in those pictures were all dark in color, and the flag behind them was the Stars and Stripes.

I'd expected the Stars and Bars, of course.

"You, uh . . ."

"That's right, Marshal. I served our Union. The same one you now serve in a different capacity."

"You aren't originally from Texas, Colonel?"

"On the contrary. I very much am from Texas. My family is from east Texas. We have been for several generations."

"But . . ."

"Not all of Texas believed in the dissolution of the Union, Marshal. Governor Sam Houston did not. Were you aware of that?"

I shook my head.

"Houston is the father of the state. And of the republic before statehood. He, and some others of us with him, could not put aside our love for the United States. We chose to stand for its preservation."

"I hadn't known about . . . That must have been mighty hard to do. Neighbors, friends, all of that."

"And families too in some instances. Yes, it was difficult. But worthwhile. After the war," he shrugged, "some of us found it more comfortable to relocate than to return to our former homes. I came here. I still do love my state, Marshal. Almost as much as I love my country. I could not have borne the thought of leaving Texas entirely."

I looked at Col. Randall Moore and found it hard to think that a man like this would be behind the murder of a deputy U.S. marshal.

But then, dammit, maybe that's what he wanted me to believe.

"Would you care for more tea, Marshal?"

"No, sir, but I thank you for the offer. Would you mind if I asked you a few more questions."

"Anything you wish."

"Thank you, sir." Not that I had anything in mind, exactly, but it seemed like the sort of thing a lawman ought to do when he's trying to run down criminals. So we sat there and jawed about this and that while the sun dropped lower and the time came on toward when this Jenson and the other Rocker M hands should be getting back to the place.

FORTY-NINE

I talked with Jenson, the four regular Rocker M hands and two brothers who'd hired on to cut and haul wood—Lord only knew where they would find it, but that's what they said they were there for—and none of them admitted to knowing anything interesting about Phylo Barnes.

Certainly none of them had any idea—or so they claimed—about why he would want to take a shot at me.

"He wasn't friendly, but he wasn't that cussed either," one of them put it. "And he was too much of a weasel to've been in such serious trouble in the past that he'd be scared of you finding out anything about him."

"A weasel?"

"Nervous. Blustery. He could be mean sometimes and nasty, but if somebody stood up face-to-face with him, he'd back off."

"Yellow son of a bitch is what Leo is sayin', Marshal," another hand put in on the subject.

"Phylo wasn't real smart either, Marshal. The truth is, we'd tease him sometimes and he wouldn't even know he was being ragged. You could make him believe most anything if you told it with a straight enough face."

"What about money?"

The cowboys shrugged. "Everybody likes that. Hardly

anybody has it. I don't think Phylo was much different than anybody else when it came to money.''

"He spent it quick as the rest of us come payday," one said.

"I wouldn't say he was broke any quicker or any later than the others," Jenson put in.

The cook, a man called Coosie of course, slapped a second steak onto my plate. If I'd known cowhands could eat this well, I might've considered honest employment back when I had a choice in such matters. "Barnes was a no-account son of a bitch," Coosie said. "His kind would backshoot a man and never think twice about it."

One of the cowboys laughed. "Tell the marshal why you didn't like Phylo, Coosie."

The cook glared at the cowboy.

"We aren't funning you, Coosie. Ben was serious. It's the sort of thing the marshal needs to know if he's trying to find out about a man."

Coosie grimaced and growled for a bit, but it seemed to be something he wanted to get off his chest anyway. "That man had no more appreciation than a boar hog does," he complained. "He ate more of my biscuits than any two other people and never once said thank you nor told me how good they are."

"Then he was a fool for sure, Coosie," I assured him, "because I've tried your biscuits my own self and can honestly say that I've never had their like before." Which was the truth. They were without question the worst darn biscuits I ever put a tooth to.

Coosie beamed at what he thought was a compliment. I gathered that Phylo Barnes hadn't been the only employee of the Rocker M outfit that was about two quarts short of a bushel.

"You want another steak, Marshal?"

"No, thanks, two is enough for me."

"If you want more, you let me know."

"Thanks."

I went back to talking with the boys from the Rocker M. I didn't really expect to learn anything definitive. That's one of the good things about low expectations. You aren't real often disappointed.

FIFTY

Jenson offered me a bunk at the Rocker M, but it wasn't all that late in the evening nor all that far back to Broad Valley. And I've had plenty enough practice at riding through the night that I don't mind it at all. I wouldn't say that I prefer it, exactly, but I certainly don't dislike it.

About an hour south of the ranch on my way back to town, though, I kinda wished I'd made a different decision. The days had gotten so pleasant and springlike that I most forgot how cold Texas can be. Now I remembered. Hadn't thought to bring my coat along when I rode out in broad daylight, nor my gloves, so I had to make do with wrapping up in my slicker. That kept the wind off but did nothing to hold the cold out.

I shivered and grumbled my way along through a moonless night. The sky was clear, though, and the stars bright and I didn't need any more than that to find my way.

It was late by the time I got back to the livery. Alex heard me come in. He poked his head out of the tack room that he used for his office and nodded when he saw who it was.

"Mind if I sleep in your straw?" I asked him. I didn't want to go and wake the Goodson family coming in so late. The women of the house had enough on their plate taking care of Carl without me making them lose sleep too.

"Straw pile or the hay, either one," Alex said.

"In that case I'll be up in the loft, and I thank you." Hay is a whole lot softer to sleep in than straw—warmer too for that matter—but a fair good many liverymen don't like anybody sleeping in it. They claim that packs it down and makes it break up and go dusty quicker than if it's left alone. Me, I've never paid all that much mind to the question. But then it's never been my hay that was being slept in. I might feel different on the subject if it was.

I hung my saddle on one of the stands Alex had in the place and draped everything else over it, including the yellow slicker that wouldn't do anything but make me feel all the colder now that there wasn't any wind to be blocked.

I curried and brushed ugly and cleaned his feet, then turned him back into his stall and gave him a couple scoops of mixed grain from the bin. Call it about three quarts at a guess. Forked a little hay into the rack for him and called it a night. I climbed the ladder into the loft and burrowed so deep into the piled hay up there that my nose was about all that was sticking out. I was still too darn cold from riding in the night air and wanted to get warm.

That loose hay did the trick just fine. In a few minutes I quit shivering and in a few more went off to sleep.

Well, I say that I went off to sleep. I wouldn't actually know.

What I do know is that I was wide-eyed and fully awake some time later when the sound of somebody whispering down below caught my attention.

The sound of the whispers carried into the hayloft clear but not quite clear enough for me to make out the actual words.

There was that and then the sound of the ladder rungs creaking as somebody climbed up toward where I was.

I lay about as still as I could manage and reached for the gunbelt that I'd taken off before I went to sleep.

For half a second I couldn't find it, and my heart commenced to thump and bang at a furious rate.

Then the grips of my pistol came to hand, cool and solid and welcome, and I lay there in the hay hoping this was just some other fella come to get some sleep.

FIFTY-ONE

"There's nobody up here." The voice sounded close. A couple feet from my head maybe.

"You're sure?" The answer from down below wasn't loud exactly, but neither of them was whispering now, just holding things down like they didn't want Alex to hear but were no longer worried about waking somebody in the loft.

Of course I could've been misjudging them completely, and if so I would be glad to apologize. But under the circumstances I favored caution instead of raising up and letting them know that there was somebody in that loft after all.

"He's back, dammit. The horse is there."

"Well, he ain't up here."

"He didn't go back to the house."

"Fine. So where the hell did he go?"

"He's got to be up there. We already looked in the straw. Look again."

I thought about thumbing the hammer back on my Colt to save half a second or so but didn't want to make the noise that even a properly oiled action will when it's cocked.

"I'm telling you, he ain't up here." The guy beside my head sounded peeved. Good for him. He shouldn't ought to let anybody order him around like that. "If you want to come up and fork through all this stuff, go ahead. Hay dust makes my nose run and gives me the sniffles. I'm coming down.''

''You're sure—''

''I said I was, di'n't I?'' the one up there with me snapped.

''Don't be so damn loud. You'll wake the old man.''

The one on the ladder didn't bother to answer, and a moment later I could hear the ladder rungs creak and groan again as he climbed back down to the barn floor.

Now that the two of them were close to one another, they went back to whispering again so that I couldn't make out what they were saying. Whatever it was they took it outside with them.

I shivered. It wasn't at all cold inside that nest of loose hay, but I shivered anyhow.

Found my holster and slid the Colt back into it.

Went to shaking so bad I was afraid my teeth were going to rattle and my heels go to drumming on the hayloft flooring. I wouldn't have wanted that. Those fellows down below might yet be close enough to hear and come back.

It might seem self-centered of me to think so, but I just couldn't escape the conclusion that it was me they'd been here looking for.

Couldn't help but think too that it wasn't peace and goodwill they had in mind were they to find me.

The horse was back. That was what they'd said. And while it was perfectly true that Alex rented out horses all the time and boarded more than just mine, there were only a few possibilities about how many would've been taken out this past evening and returned late.

And they'd said the house was watched. The Goodson house, I figured that to be.

Somebody had laid out in the brush—or whatever—and kept an eye on the Goodson house to see was I going back there to bed.

If I had, I suppose I would've been ambushed again. Shot in the back again maybe. No not maybe, probably.

Whoever it was around here that wanted me dead, they'd

already found out that it's easier to shoot me in the back than from the front.

I scowled and thought about that. And recognized of course that it wasn't really me that somebody wanted dead but Deputy Marshal Tanner. As if that made any difference now.

Damn it all, though. I was about to get tired of this. They'd already shot me once. Tried to shoot me a couple other times. And wounded poor Reverend Goodson in the process of it all.

This was really beginning to aggravate me.

I sat up and brushed the load of hay and seeds and dust off me, buckled my gunbelt on—that isn't something I generally thought of as a priority item in the mornings but was learning to change that habit—and went down the ladder.

I was hoping those two jehus were still somewhere close enough by that I could get a peep at them. I hadn't had the pleasure of getting a look at either of them yet and wanted to really bad.

Unfortunately they were neither of them in sight when I stood quiet in the shadows and peered outside the livery stable onto the street. I had no idea where they'd got to but it wasn't anyplace that I could see.

A glance at the sky told me it was coming dawn, so I must have slept longer than I'd realized before the arrival of guests woke me. For sure I felt wide awake now. Not necessarily refreshed but darn sure wide awake.

I found a few reasons to stay inside the barn for a little while. Important stuff like rolling my slicker tighter and tying it behind the cantle of my old saddle again and giving ugly another brushing. Heck, I even gave the gray some attention, though he wasn't hardly worth the bother.

I kept it up with one excuse or another until the sun was coming up and there was light enough that I didn't think I had to worry too much about assassins lurking in dark alleys.

It was still cold, but d'you know, I didn't hardly feel it when I walked out onto the main street and made my way back to the cafe where I'd first eaten here in Broad Valley.

There was a different fellow waiting table at this hour of

the morning, but the food was good and the service prompt.

And no one seemed to think it odd that I passed by two empty and perfectly good tables so I could tuck myself away into a corner where I had two solid walls behind me.

I enjoyed my breakfast just fine in the corner there, thank you.

FIFTY-TWO

If you don't think I was some kind of nervous walking from the cafe out to the Reverend Goodson's house, well guess again.

I think I spent about half my time walking backward and sideways on my way there so as to be able to see in all directions at once. Which can't be done although I did my best to manage it.

They say a horse, with eyes on the two opposite sides of its head, can move its eyes independent of one another and can see front and back at the same time if it wants to. I was envious, believe me.

I took a route that I'd never been before, cut through a couple alleys and one backyard. I was glad there weren't many trees or decorative bushes or tall standing flower beds around the houses in town, for that meant there were fewer places for a man with a rifle or shotgun to hide himself.

As it was there were too dang many. And my heart skipped a beat for every one I looked at that morning.

I got through town without anybody trying to pot me, though, and quick-walked—be damned if I'd break into a run, not for any cowardly SOB of a backshooter; unless I really knew one was around, that is—the last few rods to the back porch of the reverend's house.

I let myself in and found Sarah in the kitchen there. She

was stirring something in a steaming pot. I didn't have to see inside to know what it was, for I recognized the smell from my own recuperation in this house. She was making chicken soup.

"How's your father?"

"Much better now, thanks to you," she said.

"Me? Your poppa was shot thanks to me. That's what I've done for the Goodson family."

"He said you saved his life," Sarah said.

"More like the other way around. He seen . . . excuse me, saw . . . He saw the gunman first. He hollered and pushed me aside. The bullet he took was meant for me, Sarah. It's my fault he's hurt."

"Daddy doesn't think so."

"Yeah, but your poppa is a very charitable man."

"You're a pretty good man yourself," she said. Which made me feel kinda uncomfortable since pretty much everything she knew about me was a lie right straight from the get-go. "May I ask you something?"

"Sure."

"May I call you Riley?"

There was another name that I would've liked even better to hear coming soft off those lips, but I couldn't say anything about that. I settled for "Of course you can."

She smiled, glanced down into the soup pot to make sure it wasn't fixing to boil over or anything, then came over to me and stood so close in front of me that I could practically feel the warmth of her reaching through my shirt. I thought my heart had been jumpy just because there was a guy somewhere trying to shoot me? I hadn't had the half of it. It jumped from a walk right past the canter stage and into a ring-tailed run with Sarah being so close as she was.

And then—I couldn't hardly believe it—she went up onto her tiptoes and placed a little kiss, light and delicate as a moth's wing, on my cheek. Real close beside my mouth, though. Real close.

I could feel the heat rushing into my face and clenched both hands into fists lest I do something really dumb like grab hold of the girl and plant a sloppy wet one on her.

"Thank you for saving daddy's life, Riley."

It took me a few seconds to get my tongue under control so I could answer back. "I didn't . . . It was him, that is . . . I never . . ."

She sniffed and tossed her head. "Deny all you like. Daddy says you saved him, and I will be grateful to you for the rest of my life. So put that in your pipe and smoke it, if you please."

She went back to the stove and stirred the soup around like it was cream she was trying to whip, snatched a bowl down off the shelf with a clatter that you'd of swore should have broke the thing, then ladled up about half a bowl of that fine-smelling stuff. She put the bowl onto a tray with some other things and picked the tray up in both hands, balancing everything careful so she wouldn't spill.

"Would you open the door for me, please?"

"Of course." I did so, a mite awkwardly I guess, and she had to push past me so close that she brushed right up against me. She smelled of chicken soup but also of that flowery fragrance that I'd noted on her before sometimes. I concentrated on keeping my hands where they belonged. Which was on the door and not the girl, darn it.

Sarah drifted back toward her folks' bedroom, holding the tray high in both hands.

It occurred to me while I watched her go that during the weeks I'd spent laying about while Sarah brought soup to me and tended to me in so many ways, she'd never once had any difficulty carrying a soup tray in just one hand while she used the other to manage doors and side tables and such as that.

I thought . . . No, danggit. Sometimes a fellow is better off not thinking. I shook my head to clear such as that away, then followed behind Sarah. I needed to see Carl Goodson and thank him for what he'd done for me.

FIFTY-THREE

"If you two would please stop thanking each other for a minute, I'd like to feed him this soup before it gets cold."

"Yes, ma'am."

"Yes, dear."

Sarah took my elbow and pulled me back away from Carl's bedside so her mother could get in there and go to spooning the chicken soup into her husband.

I had to admit that Carl Goodson looked a whole lot better than I'd expected him to. I mean, this man was shot just twenty-four hours or so ago, and here he was propped up against a pile of fluffy pillows. His color looked good, his hair was combed nice and neat, and if he hadn't been in need of a shave, there wouldn't hardly have been any way to tell that things weren't entirely normal. Not just from seeing him in the bed there.

Mrs. Goodson filled him up with her good soup and a slice of bread warm from the oven—I wondered just how early a woman would have to get up in the morning so her family could enjoy fresh bread at this hour—then she handed the pretty much empty tray to Sarah and led the way out of the bedroom, leaving me behind with Carl.

"You up to me asking you a few things?," I asked.

Carl nodded. "It isn't as bad as I would have expected."

"Hurts though, doesn't it?" I knew, of course. Somewhat more than I might've liked if given my pickings on the subject. I'd been there.

"Of course. Mostly when I move."

I nodded. "You know what to do about that, I suppose."

Carl grinned. "Don't move."

"You got it." I winked at him.

"Elvira tells me you, uh, shot the man who shot me. I can't thank you for that, you know."

"No, sir, and I wouldn't want you to. It isn't something that I'm proud of."

"That isn't, shall we say, the attitude I would have expected from a man of your, um, profession."

"I can't tell you what anybody else would feel or say or do, Carl." His first name came easy to me now for some reason. "It's what I feel myself. I can tell you that much."

"His name was Barnes?"

"Yes, sir. Phylo Barnes. Did you know him?"

Carl shook his head. "I'm sure I never met him. I believe I've seen him on the street now and then. I may have even nodded or spoken to him on occasion. But I seldom venture out on Saturday nights when the ranch hands are most likely to be in town. I have my sermons to prepare. And some things I simply don't relish having to witness."

"Of course. D'you happen to know anything about the Rocker M ranch or Colonel Moore that owns it?"

"I am acquainted with the colonel. But only slightly. He has come to services on occasion. Not regularly. We've never met at what you would call a social function. The colonel tends to keep mostly to himself."

"D'you know why that would be so?"

"Of course. Colonel Moore is not a popular man among his neighbors. He fought on the wrong side in the recent war for their tastes. Perhaps you didn't know that."

I knew it, of course. I'd wondered if it made much of a difference around here. Apparently it did.

"Is there any reason . . . I don't want to step on your toes here or ask you stuff that you oughtn't to tell me . . . but is there anything you know about the colonel, something in his past say or something going on now, that would make you think he'd have cause to be afraid of the law?''

"Nothing. Quite the contrary, in fact. I don't suppose it would be betraying a confidence if I were to tell you that Colonel Moore is one of our biggest and most reliable contributors at the church.''

"I thought you said he only comes now and then.''

"I did. And that is indeed true. He participates only rarely, but the man is a regular contributor to the church. Ours is a struggling congregation, Marshal. May I call you Riley?''

"Of course.''

"This is not a prosperous community to begin with, Riley, and the people here have little to spare. And . . . how can I put this?'' He shook his head, obviously reluctant to say whatever might have come next. "Even though he doesn't feel welcome among certain members of the congregation, he has instructed Mr. Brainard at the bank to make regular disbursements into the church's account. Ten dollars on the first of every month.''

"You said he's your biggest contributor?''

"Yes, that's right.''

"And he gives ten dollars a month?''

Carl laughed. "I don't know what you assume about church finance, Riley, but a church's needs can be large and the income is very small. I don't think we could survive at all if I took a salary out of our budget.''

"You don't get paid for what you do?''

"I am paid handsomely. But not in money. For that I rely on the barbershop.''

"You surprise me,'' I admitted.

Carl shrugged. "Things will improve when the economic conditions here get better.''

"What kind of things are bad and how d'you expect them to get better?'' I asked. After all, money is the best motive for any sort of crime. Nobody knew that better than me.

"This area seems to be in something of a slump. I don't really know why. Our church had been growing, becoming stronger and larger. Slowly but surely. Or so I thought. Then some of the farms and smaller ranches failed. People moved away. Churchgoers, some of them. The congregation has been shrinking and the financial contributions even more so.''

''Why'd folks start going under? Drought? Locusts? What?''

Carl frowned. ''You know, this may sound strange to you, but I've never heard anyone say why it is they believe these things have happened. They just . . . have.''

''No special reason?'' I asked.

''No,'' he said, his own voice sounding puzzled now that he was thinking about it. ''None.''

''Did any of the folks that were leaving say anything about what happened to them?''

''Yes, several of the farm families had been very faithful members of the congregation. The Benjamins, the Loncallos, the Wenwrights, all of them came in to tell me good-bye and to say they wouldn't be back.''

''Ask for money to help them out, did they?''

''I really couldn't tell you about that, Riley.''

Which meant that they did, of course. Not that I supposed it mattered. I was just following odd thoughts and dropping them out to be looked at and chewed over. ''What did they say about why they failed? Were they bad farmers?''

''I would have to admit, Riley, that I don't know much about farms or farming. I do think I know a fair amount about people.'' He smiled. ''You, for instance. I know that you are a good man, Marshal Riley Tanner.''

I hope I didn't show how bad it made me feel to hear Carl say that. My whole situation here wasn't anything more than a bald lie, just about every word I'd ever told the man, and here he was talking nice about me like that. It made me plenty uncomfortable to hear him say it.

He noticed too. Don't think that he didn't. ''I've embarrassed you, haven't I? I'm sorry.'' It was bad enough that Carl was such a good man, but why'd he have to be perceptive too, damm it.

''You haven't said if you think they were such bad farmers that they should've failed like they did,'' I reminded him, grateful for an excuse to change the subject back to where it'd been.

"Jim Loncallo . . . perhaps I shouldn't say this, but I'm not sure he had what it takes to take barren, empty prairie and turn it into a farm. The others, though. I would have sworn that if anyone could make it on this land those families surely would have done so."

"But they all failed."

"That's right. Their crops did all right. I know they did. But they couldn't quite make ends meet. They paid too high a price for seed, perhaps, and received too little at harvest. Something on that order. They all said very much the same thing when they spoke of it, though. They just couldn't make it through on the little income they received. So they sold out and left."

"How about the new folks?" I asked. "Are they having the same troubles on those farms?"

Carl Goodson got the doggonedest curious look on him when I asked that. To the point that I prodded, "Are you all right, Carl? Is there something you want me to bring you? For the pain or like that?"

"No, I just . . . Do you know, Riley, it is the funniest thing. That is, I hadn't particularly thought of it before this very moment. But do you know . . . I don't think there are any new families on those farms."

"You told me the folks that left sold out and went."

"Yes, exactly. That's what they told me."

"But there's no one on those farms now?"

"I . . . Why, I don't believe there is. Isn't that strange?"

"Yeah. It is."

Probably not important, I thought, but for certain sure strange. I wondered why anybody would buy a farm and then just let it lie fallow like that. A farm? At least three farms. And those were only the ones Carl mentioned. There could easy be more beyond those few.

I wondered . . . Naw. There was likely nothing to it. And I sure had other things to think about right now.

Like who it was that wanted me dead. And why they wanted it.

FIFTY-FOUR

I chatted with Carl for a few minutes more, then excused myself and went out.

Out as in out of the house. I was kind of scared to. There were at least two people out there who wanted me dead. But I could either hide inside the Goodson place until something—I don't know what—changed of its own accord. Or I could go out and try to get something done.

And since it didn't look like I really had very much choice in the matter, I got my rifle from the bedroom, let Mrs. Goodson and Sarah know I was leaving and stepped out the back door.

There were only two doors leading into the Goodson house. I was wishing there were more so I would have more choices and maybe be able to confuse anybody that wanted to shoot me coming or going.

Since I already knew there were two doors and two or more men to cover them, well, I didn't feel real secure when I stepped out into the bright sun of mid-morning.

Fortunately I wasn't molested. I stood there on the stoop looking around for a minute or so but didn't see anything suspicious, and after a bit I relaxed just a little and went on out to the street.

The county building—it wasn't much of a building, not

a regular courthouse or anything, but it's what they had and I'm sure they were proud of it—was four blocks away and although the day was nice and mild and pleasant now that the sun was up, I was sweating pretty good by the time I got to Sheriff Frake's office.

The sheriff was in and, I was pleased to see, so was Mayor Tolliver, who'd said early on that he and the other town fathers stood ready to help me. Well, I could sure use some help.

I did all the howdying and hand shaking and stuff that was expected, then hung my hat on a peg and accepted the cup of coffee Herb Frake offered.

"What can we do for you, Marshal?" George Tolliver asked.

"For one thing, mister mayor, your good sheriff here can make up another report about somebody trying to kill me."

That got the reaction I'd expected from the both of them. Tolliver looked positively shocked. The sheriff seemed interested. Both men leaned forward in their chairs, and I told them about my experience when I woke up.

"You didn't get a look at either of them?" the sheriff wanted to know.

"No, I'm sorry to say that I didn't. The thing is, I figured if I could peep out and see him then he could see me right back, and as I didn't know which way his gun might be pointing, I kept still as a bunny in briars."

"You heard two voices though, is that right?"

"I know there was two of them, but I don't think there was more than that. They didn't have any reason to think they were being overheard, not once the one on the ladder decided there wasn't anybody up there in the loft with him. Alex sleeps pretty sound. Those two killers came in and left, then I got up and left too. We all of us made some noises, but Alex never heard any of it. No, I think if there'd been a third man I would have heard him, one way or another." I frowned.

"Is there something else?" Frake asked.

"Yeah. I was just thinking . . . I'm pretty sure there is a third man someplace. He wasn't at the livery this morning, but I'd say there's at least one more around here somewhere that's involved."

"Why would you think that?"

"It's something that happened when I was on my way here. Three men jumped me. Chased me quite a ways and tried to shoot me. I hadn't particularly made a connection between what happened and this. I mean, I just thought it was a robbery attempt gone wrong. Something like that. But there was for sure three of them. And now that I think of it . . . I didn't get a real close look at any of them, mind, as I had other things I was paying attention to at the time . . . but now that I think back on what I saw of them and what Phylo Barnes looked like . . . I don't think Barnes was part of that bunch. Which means if there's a connection here then there's at least three live men that're involved."

"You never mentioned that incident before," the sheriff said.

I shrugged. "Didn't think there was need to."

"You say they shot at you?"

Killed me too, dang 'em. I wanted to add that but of course didn't. "From horseback. They chased awhile, then I ducked into some boulders with a good solid cliff behind me. Once I had my rifle and a rest to shoot from, I could've picked them off pretty as a turkey at the county fair. They saw that and weren't foolish enough to try and rush me. Once they saw I had the upper hand, they turned tail and went back the way they'd come.

"I hadn't thought all that much about it, but . . . I bet they're the ones still after me. You, uh, don't know of three strangers showing up in this neighborhood lately, do you, Sheriff?"

"No, I don't. Of course cowboys drift in and out, but I don't know of any three coming in together. How about you, George?"

His Honor the mayor shook his head. "No, I haven't heard of anyone like that. I wish I could help out."

"Yes, sir, well, so do I. Oh. Before I forget, Sheriff, did you learn anything yesterday?"

He looked puzzled for a moment. Then comprehension smoothed the wrinkles out of his forehead, and Frake gave me an apologetic little smile. "No. Sorry. I should have mentioned it right away, but we got sidetracked."

"What's this, Herb?" Tolliver asked.

"Yesterday Marshal Tanner asked me to check around with the people here. They do know me better than a new-comer, of course. We were curious about Phylo Barnes's last night in town. It seems certain someone hired him to murder the marshal, and we wondered who he might have been seen with the evening before the shooting."

"You didn't learn anything?" I asked.

"No, I'm sorry. If Barnes spent any time in town that evening, he wasn't seen doing it. Not by anyone I could locate anyway, and I asked in all the places one would think he might visit."

"Well, I thank you for trying." I stood, returned my empty coffee cup to the table beside the tiny potbelly stove where the pot sat and retrieved my hat.

"What will you do next, Marshal?" Tolliver asked.

I picked up the Winchester carbine I'd propped against the wall and shrugged. "I'm not sure where to turn next," I admitted. "I know I'd feel a lot better facing three men out in the open than here in town where they can creep up on me. What I think I'll do is ride out and hope they follow. Maybe if I can draw them out I can take down one or two. Alive if possible. That would sure be a big help."

"Where will you ride out to?" the mayor asked.

"Heck, I dunno. Doesn't make much difference, I expect. I'll look for terrain that I think could give me the advantage. Then we'll see what happens from there."

"Good luck, Tanner. I mean that," the sheriff said in a solemn tone of voice.

I grinned at him. "Thanks. Meantime whyn't you ask around town some more? Maybe somebody saw those two jehus on the street just before dawn this morning or mayhap you'll yet find someone that has something to say about Phylo Barnes."

"I'm sure if anyone did know anything about Barnes they would step up and say so. The people of this town are very upset about Reverend Goodson being wounded. He's a well-received man here."

"Ayuh, no wonder. He's a good man, all right. Well, thank you for the coffee, gents. I'll see you both later, I'm sure." I touched the brim of my hat and went outside again.

Nobody shot at me. I took that as a good sign.

FIFTY-FIVE

Alex was not what you might call an early riser. When I got back to the livery stable, it was nine, maybe even going on ten o'clock I'd say, and Alex still looked sleepy-eyed and slow.

Hadn't shaved either, but then there were probably an awful lot of fellows who'd be looking bristly and scratchy until Carl was up and around again. After all, he was the town's only barber and a lot of the men in Broad Valley would depend on him for their shaves.

"Sleep well, did you?" he greeted me.

"Well enough," I told him, which was the truth. It was after the sleeping was done with that I'd had my worries, but none of that was his fault and I didn't bother bringing it up to him.

"Going out again today, are you, Marshal?"

"I expect I will, Alex."

"You want me to saddle the gray for you this time?"

"That sounds good." It was only natural that he would expect me to use Riley Tanner's gray horse. About the only reason a man might want to encumber himself with more than one horse to feed would be so he could swap off the use of them and keep them fresh.

And anyway now that he'd mentioned it, it occurred to me that if there were any bullets flying around today I'd sure rather it be the gray horse that was put in harm's way than old ugly.

My own cayuse is plain and nothing to brag on, but I'm used to the dumb creature and wouldn't like to see him shot.

Alex got the gray out and clipped him into the crossties, then started working on his feet while I fetched my kak from the stand where I'd dropped it last night. When the liveryman got done with a little quick brushing, I strapped everything where it ought to be and slid my carbine into the boot under my right stirrup.

"Hunting for bear today, Marshal?" Alex observed.

"Why d'you ask?"

He inclined his head toward the scabbard. "You didn't carry that with you yesterday."

"Oh. Yeah." I shrugged and said, "You never know when you might get hungry for coyote stew."

Alex chuckled. "It's one way to put it."

He didn't ask where I was going. Which was just as well since I hadn't any idea about that myself. I gathered up my reins and stepped into the saddle. Hunched low in the seat and got ready to hang on in case the gray was feeling cranky after a good rest and now a complete stranger setting atop him.

The horse just stood there, and I relaxed a mite.

I happened to think that I really ought to have a direction to take. Especially in the event somebody came around asking Alex which way I'd gone. Not only would I want him able to tell them, I'd want him able to tell me afterward just who it was that did the asking.

Since I already knew the way to the Rocker M, and folks would be expected to know that I did, I couldn't go back there again. Not and ask Alex for directions, I couldn't.

"Tell me, Alex, do you happen to know some of the farm families that've pulled stakes and moved on? Carl Goodson mentioned a couple places to me. Let me see can I think of the names. He talked about several."

"Bannister?" he suggested.

I shook my head.

"Loncallo?"

"That's one. And another . . . let me see . . . Bin . . . , Ben . . . , uh . . ."

"Cody Benjamin?"

"That would be another, yes."

Alex rattled off a couple other names that didn't sound familiar. Which didn't necessarily mean that Carl hadn't mentioned them, just that I didn't happen to remember them.

"What about them people?" Alex asked.

"I was wondering where they lived. Where their farms were."

"Oh, that's easy enough. They all lived east of town. You know the road that goes out past the church?"

"Uh huh." I'd come in on that road.

"Well, you ride out that way about two miles. You'll see wagon tracks leading off to the north."

"Uh huh."

"The first track you see . . . I wouldn't call it a road but maybe it will be someday . . . that first track leads to the Whitworth place. The next one after that would be Jim Loncallo's old place. Then Benjamin next in line. Johnson after that, I think. I can't remember for sure the exact order from there. There's a right smart of quarter-section and half-section farms strung out in that direction from there. You'll see another track every half mile or so from here on down to Meachum."

"Meachum," I repeated. "That a farm, is it?"

Alex gave me an odd look. "No, it's a town."

"I didn't recall."

"Yeah, well, anyway, those people you mentioned, them and a bunch more like them, they most of them live out in that same direction. Or did. Some of them have already gone belly-up. But then you knew that already, didn't you?"

"You're a big help, Alex."

"Anytime."

"You say the Loncallo farm is up the second wagon track?"

"That's right. 'Bout a half mile past Bob Whitworth's. You can't miss it."

I grinned down at him from the gray's back. "Sure I can. But I'll try not to." I tipped my hat to him and squeezed the gray gently. I don't care to use spurs on a horse if I don't have to.

The gray turned his head half around as if to say he'd forgot I was up there. But now he remembered.

Dang old snide dropped his muzzle, blew a spray of snot thick enough to form a rainbow if we'd been out in the sun and set real serious about the task of trying to get me off his back.

For a little while there I wasn't sure if we were going to end up killing him, me or Alex, who was kept mighty busy keeping out of the way. But after some snorting and bucking—he didn't have room enough, thank goodness, to really get into it—we worked it out which one of us was going to take charge of the other.

After that he settled down and walked out of the barn just as meek as a lapdog and twice as pretty, the useless damn thing. Riley Tanner might've been some punkin as a lawman, but he sure hadn't known horses.

"G'day," I said as we passed out from the doorway. I touched my hat brim to Alex and got a smile in return.

FIFTY-SIX

I'd only asked directions to those farms because I didn't know of anything else around Broad Valley *to* ask for. But it worked out fine, especially as they lay east of town.

The livery was on the far west end and the church to the east, which meant that I was going to have to pass clean through town from end to end. That couldn't have been any better, especially since I was wanting to call attention to myself in the hope that one or more of those jaspers would come after me.

Just to make it all the more likely that I'd be seen—and, all right I admit it, to make myself less of a slow and easy target here in the closer confines of the town limits—I put the gray horse into a high lope and went sailing through Broad Valley quick as a drunk cowboy with trail pay lying heavy in his pockets.

The sound of the gray's feet turned heads and brought doors open the whole length of the place. Even Sheriff Frake and the mayor came out of the county building to see what the running was about, and I don't doubt that the sheriff would have called me down and written me out a citation except for me being a deputy U.S. marshal and all that.

I sat tall, leaning back in the saddle and enjoying the air in my face, and saluted the sheriff with a wink and a nod when I went by him. Of course him and the mayor already knew what I was up to, but I'll bet the rest of the town took notice and wondered.

That was just exactly fine by me too.

I drummed fast right on by the church. Sarah was walking toward the road from the direction of the house. She saw me and waved, and I waved back, remembering the first time I'd seen her, as she was on her way home from someplace.

Oh, my. I tried to put Sarah Goodson out of mind. It wouldn't do me any good to think thoughts about a decent girl like that.

The gray wasn't much of a horse but his gait was smooth enough, and he felt all right under me. I kept him running even after Broad Valley was well behind. Dang thing had been getting too sassy cooped up in a stall all the time and needed to have some of the vinegar worked out of him.

I held him to the pace until he started to break a light sweat, then dropped him down to a jog. The gray didn't have anyway near so nice a road gait as ugly did. But then not many horses did, and I hadn't really expected it.

By the time the gray had the sass worked out of him, I came to the first set of wheel ruts leading left, just like Alex said. Past those a half mile or so I came to another set and reined the gray up them.

This one was supposed to be the Lo . . . Loca . . . Ah, it didn't matter what the name of these people was. There wasn't anybody lived here now anyway, right?

I bumped the gray horse into a lope again.

FIFTY-SEVEN

There's something forlorn and almighty lonely about an abandoned farm. I'd seen them before a time or two, and I don't like it. A farm without life to it is a shameful thing. Someone hoped and dreamed there and the dreams all died.

This farm was like that. It was a sign of failure but more than that it showed a man's defeat.

One of my own earliest memories was of riding in a wagon and looking back at an empty farm that wasn't so awful unlike this one.

My father'd never gotten over his failure on that farm. I wondered if Jim-Something of the family that'd been here would ever recover and be a whole and happy man again. I kinda hoped that he would.

Anyway, I rode up on the place. It wasn't terribly far off the road. Three-fourths of a mile or thereabouts. Like so much in this part of the country, I hadn't been able to see it from far off because of the rolling of the ground. Most of the rises were so slight you couldn't hardly make them out, but they were there sure enough and some of them you never even recognized until you came up on top of them and could unexpected-like see off toward the horizon again.

There wasn't so very much to see once I did get there. There was a set of pens that would have held the pulling horses, maybe a cow or two and some pigs. The fences were already starting to fall down now that there was no one left to keep them in good repair.

I could see a dugout off past the livestock pens. I guessed that would have been the first excuse for a house on the place. Dugouts are quick and easy to make and don't cost anything.

The farmhouse that replaced the dugout wasn't all that much of a house itself. It wasn't but a soddy, built using slabs of plowed prairie sod as if they were building blocks, laying them up in overlapping courses like you would with brick and mortar. But weight and their own mud was enough to hold the sod pieces together. Add a roof of saplings, more sod and buy just enough lumber to frame the door, maybe a window or two, and you had yourself a house. They leaked mud when it rained and were host to all manner of bugs, mice and other vermin. But they were warm in winter and cool in summer and housed many a family when they were new on their land and too poor to pay for much in the way of comfort.

I stepped down off the gray—no point waiting around for an invitation here—and tied the horse to one of the fence posts that was still upright.

I could see a place on the ground that showed where a small barn or large shed would have been. Whatever it was, it wasn't there now. Probably somebody, a neighbor or whatever, came along and helped himself to it, either carting away the whole shebang or maybe taking it apart and pilfering one board at a time.

There was another place, much smaller and also vacant now, where I guessed the outhouse would have been. The dump hole was filled in now, probably to make sure nobody missed seeing it and fell in.

Same thing with the well. It looked like they'd had a shallow well with a weighted pole to drop and then lift a bucket. All that rig was missing now too but I could see where it had been.

Off to the north and east I could see bare ground, innocent of the native grasses that would have been here since the old-timey buffalo days and who knows how much further back in time.

Jim-Somebody was here long enough to plow the ground and turn the grass under. He got a crop, could've been several. Now he was gone and so was the grass. The ground looked naked without it, and though it was coming spring there was no one to plow and plant and tend to this earth.

Like I said. It was one lonely, empty son of a bitch. I didn't much like looking at it.

I left the horse tied there and went to look inside the house.

It was empty, of course. I hadn't expected anything else. But you can't hardly come across an abandoned place and not look inside. You know?

There were patches of leather nailed to the door frame to show where a door had been hung. The door was gone now.

The house faced south. There was one window facing south and another to the east. Nothing, of course, on the north side or the west, where the worst of the cold and wind and snow would come from. Jim-Something hadn't been a first-class farmer, but he wasn't stupid.

The floor was dirt, packed and smoothed and near as hard as stone. I guessed Mrs. Jim-Something probably mixed clay with cow manure, got the mess good and wet and used it to pave her floor. It doesn't sound very nice, but it dries slick and hard and actually makes a pretty good floor that will last a long time and can be kept swept clean.

It wasn't clean now. Bits of this and that had blown in through the open door and windows or worked their way out of the layer of dried grass laid up as part of the roof, so now the floor was dirty and unkempt. I bet Mrs. Jim-Something would've been sad to see what had become of her place now.

There were some flat stones where a stove would have been. A hole in the roof for the stovepipe. A couple pegs left driven into the mud-plastered sod walls.

That was about it. Not a scrap of cloth or busted furniture left behind for whoever came after.

If anybody ever did. Looking at the place now, it was

hard to imagine somebody wanting to buy this place and live in this house and farm this land.

I suppose somebody might could look at all this and see opportunity where Jim-Somebody found failure.

But it sure wouldn't be me.

I shivered a mite although it wasn't particularly cold, then turned and went back out into the spring sunshine.

FIFTY-EIGHT

Nobody seemed interested in shooting at me that afternoon.

Now, generally that is the sort of comment a person can make with some degree of satisfaction. Certainly I'd never before found myself wanting someone to come along with lethal intent.

But this day, well, this one time I would've welcomed seeing those jehus come. I wanted a look at them. More than that, danggit, I wanted a shot at them.

They'd had their chances at me, I figured. Now it would be only fair for me to take a turn.

I sat there, comfortable in the doorway of the old dugout with the sun on me to keep warm with and sod walls behind to keep the wind off, and waited the whole rest of the day.

Come sundown nobody had showed up, and I was cramped and cold and more than a little bit sour of disposition too. I stood up and stamped my feet to get some circulation back, then picked up my Winchester and went back to the gray horse.

I was still leery of those unknown murderers, though, thinking while I was sitting in the mouth of the dugout somebody might have snuck up behind the place where I couldn't see and be waiting out there. So I was cautious and careful and nervous as a cat with no whiskers.

No need to be. My assassins must have been taking the day off after a hard night of laying in ambush.

I shoved the Winchester into the saddle boot, collected my reins and climbed onto the gray.

There was no excitement this time when I moved him off. He'd already had the green taken off him for this day and acted polite enough. And I never hold it against a horse for finding out how things lie. This one knew now that I wouldn't take anything off him, and he acted agreeable enough. I still didn't like the animal all that much. His gaits weren't the best and his bottom was suspect. But I'd ridden worse. I could say that much for him.

Seemed pointless to ride all the way back to the road just to turn straight west to Broad Valley, so I pointed the gray toward where the sun was busy disappearing and headed out.

I could tell easy when I passed off the quarter section that had belonged to Jim-Something and onto the neighbor's ground.

Alex had said there was a string of failed farms running off to the east from Jim-Something's land, but this outfit was still going. I crossed a field that was fresh plowed but not yet planted and then another slightly smaller field that wasn't only prepared, it was already planted. There was yet light enough that I could see specks of green beginning to sprout in a broadcast pattern. Considering the time of year and the way the seed was spread, I figured the field to be oats or maybe barley.

I say I crossed it but actually what I did was rein the gray around it and then turn west again when I was by the oat field. You can't hurt much by crossing through a field planted in rows or hills, not if you're paying attention, but there's no way to avoid causing damage if you blunder through a broadcast field.

Just the other side of the oats I came up on the back side of another set of buildings pretty much like Jim-Something's had been, the difference being that people still lived here and the place was still being farmed.

What I found sad was to discover that there wasn't a

whole awful lot of difference in appearance between this place and that of Jim-Something.

The one behind me looked ghostly and empty.

This one just looked . . . dreary. Tired and poor and miserable.

Lordy, I wouldn't have been a dry land farmer. Not for anything.

I got to feeling sorry for myself sometimes, what with being chased and a price on my head and everything.

But it sure as fire beat this.

I guided the gray into the yard and pulled him to a stop beside the well.

FIFTY-NINE

Two small boys, one of them six or seven and the other eight or nine, came running out of the house to greet me. "Who are you, mister?" "Do you want some water, mister?" "Did you come for supper?" "If you stay for supper, Mama will cook meat, mister."

There were only the two of them. They sounded like more.

I stepped down off the gray, and the taller of the boys took the reins out of my hand.

"Do you want me to water your horse for you, mister? I know how."

I nodded. "That'd be nice, son, thanks."

A girl came out of the house too. She was young. Fourteen or fifteen, I'd guess, and likely at the stage where she was right now the prettiest she ever would be her whole life long. She didn't have much to look forward to if that was so. She had a jaw like the useful end of a spade and eyes set kind of close together. She was barefoot and her dress looked like it had been handed down more than once already and was near to the end of its usefulness.

But of course I took my hat off and nodded polite as I knew how. "Evenin', miss."

"Put the gentleman's horse up," the girl instructed briskly. Then she gave me a smile and a sort of little curtsy and said, "Mama said I should tell you you're welcome to stay for supper."

I was hungry, that was a fact. And I had some money in my pants. It wasn't like I couldn't pay for a meal. I got the idea these folks could use a mite of cash in hand unexpected.

"Please tell your mama I'd be pleased to stay."

The girl smiled so bright she almost looked nice. She bobbed her head and gathered up her skirts and ran back to the house.

The boys grinned at one another, and I recalled the least one saying that if they had company they'd have meat for the meal. Heck, I knew how that was. I let them tend to the gray horse while I went off through the yard toward where I could see a man walking in behind a mule.

He had just the one mule on the place apparently. At least I didn't see any horses. There was a fresh cow in a pen but no calf in with her. There were half a dozen pigs—actually five when I got close enough to see them better—in a sty out past the storage shed.

The man was barefoot and bare headed and wore an overcoat against the chill of the evening. The mule was in harness but not pulling anything. Whatever he'd been using today, plow or rake or drag, he'd left in the field to pick up with tomorrow. The man walked with the driving lines draped over his shoulder, but the mule didn't need any driving. It knew where it was going.

The older boy was already coming with a bucket of water to pour for the mule in the same pen that held the cow. The man turned the mule over to his son, then pulled out a kerchief and carefully wiped his hand before he came over and offered me to shake.

"Whitworth's my name, friend. Bob Whitworth."

"Riley Tanner." The name was coming easier to me now that I'd been using it awhile. It still didn't sound natural, of course. But it was easier for me to get it out without making a face and acting like I ought to spit.

We shook hands, and Bob Whitworth said, "You're the federal marshal."

"Word gets around."

"It isn't every day somebody gets shot around here. I'm pleased to see you're feeling better now. We prayed for you after we heard what happened."

"That's mighty nice of you, Mr. Whitworth."

"Bob," he corrected. "Come inside, Marshal. You'll stay for supper? We'd be proud to have you."

"It'd be my pleasure, Bob."

The man smiled. "Good. We'll tell my missus."

"Your daughter already carried that message," I said.

"That would be Abby." He beamed with pride.

"Yes, sir," I said. I hadn't known the girl's name. Hadn't cared either.

"Come around here, Marshal. Toby and Ben will take care of the animals. We've a washstand and soap at the side of the house there, and if I know my Lucy there's a clean towel hanging there by now. She will have slipped out to do that soon as she saw you coming." He laughed and led the way.

A contented man, Bob Whitworth, I thought. Content with what he had. Proud of his family and of what he'd built here. I couldn't say that I envied him. But I did admire him.

And there was indeed a clean towel hanging beside the washbasin and a fresh dish of soap there too.

SIXTY

"It's not but pot luck, Marshal. I hope it will satisfy."

"If smell is any way to judge, ma'am, it will more than satisfy. It smells wonderful."

"Help yourself, Marshal. Don't be shy."

"Yes, ma'am." I took a ladle full of the steaming pot pie, taking mostly broth and dumplings and leaving the bits of tender red ham in the pot for the kids. Water and flour are cheap enough, so I didn't feel bad about taking them.

I grabbed right off for my spoon, then felt more than a little embarrassed when I saw the rest of the family sitting there waiting until all were served. When they were and the big pot was nearly empty, the children clasped their hands together while their parents held hands. All of them closed their eyes and bowed their heads.

"Lucy," Bob Whitworth said, "would you say our blessing this evening, please?"

The aroma of the pot pie tickled my nose while Mrs. Whitworth gave a prayer out loud. It was lengthy but, I was sure, heartfelt. It ran long on the thanks end of things, including for the blessing of having me as a guest at their table. It was nice of her. But then the Whitworths as a bunch seemed nice, and I would have to say that I liked them.

Bob seemed happy with his lot in life, hard though I

thought it to be. His wife seemed just as content.

And she was a plenty good cook. I could attest to that in any court of law. The broth had little golden globs of ham fat floating in it, and the square-cut dumplings were chewy and delicious, the sort of meal that would stick to a man's ribs for hours after. There wasn't anything fancy about the meal nor about the house it was served in, but I looked at these folks and saw what people meant when they talked about "honest citizens." I figured the Whitworths were the model for that term or darn sure could be.

"We're out of coffee right now, Marshal, but we have milk or buttermilk to offer."

"I generally like water with my meals if it's all the same to you, ma'am."

"Of course, Marshal. Abby, would you get the gentleman something to drink please?"

"I want buttermilk, fat face."

"Me too. I want buddermilk too."

"Toby! Mind your manners. And Ben, we don't need your comments either."

"Yes, Papa."

"Yes, Papa."

Both boys struggled to look properly contrite.

Abby made a face and stuck her tongue out at her brothers. Where her folks couldn't see her doing it, of course. She smiled real sweet when she brought me my cup of cool water.

Like I said. Fine family, the Whitworths. I liked them a lot.

SIXTY-ONE

After supper I walked outside with Bob while Lucy Whitworth and the kids cleaned up indoors. He had a pipe of something that didn't smell like regular tobacco. Some substitute he picked himself, I guessed. It looked to me like the Whitworths, nice though they were, were headed to about the same state Jim-Something and those others reached already.

I suppose it might've been impolite of me, but I was curious. Not that I know all that much about farms and farming. Not really, my interests having, you might say, diverged from that some little time back. But judging from what little I did know, Bob Whitworth seemed a pretty good farmer as well as a pretty good man. So I put politeness aside and asked the question that was vexing me.

"I know a lot of your neighbors have sold out and gone, Bob. Yet this looks like pretty good ground to me. How come it's so much harder for a man to make it here than, say, up in Kansas?"

"Marshal, if I knew the answer to that one maybe Jim Loncallo, Cody Benjamin and the rest might have been able to get by. They were good neighbors. I miss them. Would have done anything I could to keep them here on their farms, but to tell you the truth I'm not sure Lucy and me will make it through another season."

"Surely you know what the problem is," I insisted. "Are you getting short yields?"

"No, I'm not. Pretty good ones, in fact. My yields on oats, corn and barley are all well above the averages they report in this part of the country. Cody's were about average, I think. Jim's a little below. But not so bad that I would've expected him to go under."

"High debt?" I asked. Often a man will pay more than ground is worth and can't take enough out of it to keep his family and pay off a debt too.

"Dollar and a quarter an acre," he said.

"That can't be it then," I agreed.

"It's just . . . Can I call you Riley? You've sat at our table." He smiled. "That means you aren't a stranger anymore."

"You bet," I told him. Really I like being on first-name basis with folks, but I wasn't so accustomed to being known as Riley that I felt like asking people to call me that.

"You can believe I've thought about this aplenty, Riley. And it just seems like . . . like there's never quite enough to go around. Like things ought to stretch but somehow just never do. Almost. But not quite."

I grunted but didn't have anything to contribute to this good man's observations.

"When you figure in the cost of seed, then the poor prices we've gotten for our harvests . . . it just doesn't quite stretch as far as a man would expect."

"Prices been off, have they?" I knew wheat was strong and had been for the past couple years. But that was up in Kansas. Not only did I have no idea at all about how Texas prices compared with the ones I was used to from up home, I hadn't ever had any particular cause to note what the other grain crops sold for nowadays.

"Yes, they dropped about two, maybe three years ago and haven't recovered. Yet seed grain stayed high. If anything it went up a little."

"That doesn't make much sense," I said.

Bob shrugged. "Neither does farming." He grinned. "Maybe there's a good reason why old Cain was jealous of his rancher brother Abel."

I laughed. "You could be onto something there. Ever think about changing profession?"

"No. Not even if I could afford the land it would take."

"Aw, land is free, isn't it? Homestead your water and use free range for the grazing. Isn't that the way a man gets into the ranching business?"

Bob gave me an odd sort of look. "You, uh, you aren't from Texas, are you, Riley?"

"No. Why'd you ask?"

"When Texas went into the Union, the state kept all the public land for itself, and it's all private now. Well, except for some useless dry land further west, that is. There's still some state-owned ground out that way. But not around here. Here if you want land you buy it. Everything for a hundred miles in any direction from here is deeded and recorded."

"I hadn't known that," I admitted. "Even the big ranches?"

He nodded. "Even them. If a man wants a big chunk here, the easiest way is to inherit it. Either that or be awful rich to begin with."

"I see." I wondered about Colonel Moore. He hadn't inherited. Not here, he hadn't. He said he was from east Texas. He must have had money, though. And being a Unionist he wouldn't have lost his during Reconstruction. I wondered how that must sit with his Southron neighbors. Not very well would've been my guess on the subject.

"It's a shame about your neighbors," I said as I was still thinking about that too. "I heard they were able to sell, though. Is that right?"

"Yes, they were. Of course all they got back was the worth of the land itself. Years of sweat never show up on a fee-simple deed."

"How come the new owners haven't taken possession?" I asked.

"I don't know that they will. The buyer was a land and cattle company. I suppose they intend to let the ground go back to grass, and that will be that."

I frowned. "But it won't," I said.

"How's that?"

"You can't plow grass under and then expect to have grass grow back again. I've seen it over in eastern Kansas and Missouri and like that. Crop land that lies fallow won't come back to grass."

"Surely given a few years . . ."

"No, Bob," I told him emphatically, "I tell you I've seen that my own self in a couple different places. And those were better watered than around here. More rain and darker soil. If range grasses wouldn't grow back there, I'm certain they'd never come back here. Not on their own, they wouldn't. Of course a man could broadcast seed, I suppose. Put on some pulverized bonemeal and find a way to water it so he could get some roots down before the wind and the birds and mice took all his seed away. But short of that . . . No, I'm telling you. I've seen it. Range grass just won't come back once the sod is turned over."

It was Bob's turn to frown. "Then why would a land and cattle company want those farms?"

"Darned if I know. But I can tell you this. It isn't to let them go back to grass for grazing land."

Bob sucked on the stem of his pipe until all he could get out of the bowl was a wet, bubbly rattle. Then he knocked the dottle out against a fence post and said, "I expect we can go back in now if you like. It's coming chill."

"Sure."

"You're welcome to spend the night, Riley." He smiled. "My Lucy cooks a fine breakfast."

And the truth is that I'd been hoping for exactly such an invite. It had occurred to me early on that if I went back to town tonight there was a good chance there'd be another ambush waiting for me, at the Goodson house or the livery stable or both. Waiting for morning to go back would tire out whoever wanted to shoot me and would give me daylight to keep watch by too.

"I'd be pleased," I told Bob. More, in fact, than he could possibly know. "I do have one thing to ask of you, though."

"If it's in our power to give, Riley, you've got it."

"Promise?"

"Ayuh, I do."

I smiled. "Good. In that case I'll agree to stay. And you have to agree to let the government pay you for my meals and lodging."

"But . . ."

"No, I won't hear any buts about it. You said you'd grant my boon if you could, an' this you surely can. Besides, it won't be me that's paying. It will be the government."

That was a lie but this time not one that I minded. After all, sometimes a man simply has to lie. And he needs to stay in practice if he wants to be ready for the important occasions.

"Since you put it that way, Riley . . . all right. We'll take your money. But I want you to know that you're as welcome without it."

I smiled. "Heck, I already knew that, Bob. You didn't have to say it."

SIXTY-TWO

You know all those stories about passing strangers and the farmer's daughter? Well, it's a good thing I never believed any of them. And would have been nothing but upset and embarrassed if I'd had any reason to change that conviction after spending a night in the Whitworths' shed.

I slept warm and comfortable thanks to a thick quilt that'd been made by Lucy Whitworth's mother. This trip out of town I'd remembered to bring a coat and carbine but hadn't thought to pack my sougan, which I suppose was just as well because it would have tipped the ambushers not to waste their time waiting up late for me.

The only company I had through the night was some small critter—a mouse, I would guess—skittering around on the far side of the sweet smelling grass hay I bedded down in.

Even so I had some trouble first dropping off. My eyes were closed but I kept seeing Sarah Goodson in front of me.

I wouldn't say that I objected to the view.

Come morning I had a breakfast of flapjacks, oat porridge and an herb tea that darn near tasted drinkable. I have no idea what it was but it wasn't apt to put the coffee people out of business.

Afterward the boys saddled the gray for me and I found

a moment to get Mrs. Whitworth aside. I was pretty sure Bob would have wised up to the fact there was something not quite right with my idea of the going rate for government accommodations, but most women are too practical to ask awkward questions. I gave the lady of the house a ten-dollar eagle and told her I'd write it off on an expense voucher.

Hey, if I could just sign my name for ugly's feed and lodging, why the heck not for my own? Made good enough sense to me.

I thanked the grown folks and got a smile from Abby and a handshake from Toby and, most unexpected, a hug around the neck from the least one. I couldn't remember the last time I'd ever been hugged by anybody.

Well, okay, maybe I could. But it wasn't the sort of thing a person looks back on with any sort of pride, if you know what I mean. This here one was the real thing, and it kind of touched me.

I turned around and scrambled quick onto the gray's back and reined him away from there.

It was barely coming daybreak when I rode out of the Whitworths' yard, and was still early in the day when I got back to town.

I left the road as soon as I came in sight of the steeple on Carl Goodson's church, dropped south a little way and came up onto the house from a direction I didn't think would be expected even if somebody was persistent enough to still be expecting me.

Which I didn't find in any case. Broad Valley was up and around, and there weren't any assassins hiding in anybody's flower patch.

I tied the gray to the Goodson's backyard pump and went in. Carl was feeling good enough that he said he'd be able to preach.

"Is it Sunday already?"

Sarah laughed. "This is Friday. Daddy has until Sunday morning to heal some more. And he won't have to stand the whole time. We'll help him up the steps and set out a chair for him to sit in beside the pulpit. Will you help us, Marshal? Please?"

Marshal. There it was. There were a dozen or so folks around town by now who were comfortable calling me Riley. The only one I really wanted to hear that familiarity from wasn't so inclined even though she'd asked permission once already. I gathered she'd given it a try and decided it didn't fit so good. Oh, well. I didn't deserve better than that. Considering.

"Count on it," I said.

Heck, I would help Sarah if she asked me to put a rope on the moon and drag it down to where she could hack off a chunk of green cheese. But I didn't say that. Not out loud, I didn't.

"Is there anything I can do now?" I offered.

"Not unless you know how to cut hair and give shaves." Sarah giggled. "Half the men in town look like they're starting to grow beards now that Daddy is laid up and can't work."

I fingered my own chin, which was also bristly with several days' accumulation of whiskers. Like most men, I didn't own a razor of my own. Good thing too or I'd've saved some lawman a lot of work before now and cut my own throat. I've known fellows who could get up in the morning, splash cold water on their cheeks and proceed to shave themselves. No mirror or anything. They'd flip open their razor, maybe strop the blade alongside their boots a lick or three and then go to scraping. By feel alone. And hardly lose any blood in the process. Me, I can't shave myself even if I'm stone sober and have a mirror to work with. So yeah, I was willing to accept the idea that the men of Broad Valley would be getting kind of scruffy-looking by now. Me among them.

"You say this is Friday?" I asked, changing the subject.

"All day long," Sarah confirmed.

"Then the county building would be open," I said.

"Yes, of course."

I nodded and thanked her.

"Will you be back for lunch, Ma—" She paused. "Not Marshal. Riley." She smiled at me. Lordy, but I liked that. "You did say I could call you that. Do you remember?"

"I remember," I said.

"Good. Will you be back for lunch, Riley?"

I hadn't thought about it. Didn't have to study on it very long either. "I'll be back."

"I'll have a place laid for you."

I looked at her for a moment. It was something I liked doing anyway. "I won't be late," I promised.

It was not my intention to lie to her, of course.

SIXTY-THREE

"The sheriff was around a little while ago asking about you," Alex said as he took the gray horse from me. If it'd been ugly, I would have wanted to do the brushing and hoof cleaning myself, but as it was only the gray, I wasn't so fussy.

"I'll stop by and see him then, thanks."

"Anytime." Alex's attention was on the horse. I could've been making faces and dancing a jig; I doubt he would have noticed. He was already busy, starting in with a hard comb to loosen any dried sweat on the animal's back. Obviously this was a man who cared about what he was doing. I felt like ugly was in good hands here.

"Mind if I store some stuff here?" I asked. I was thinking of my saddlebags and sougan. Just in case. If I kept them here, I wouldn't have to worry about anybody seeing me tote them all the way through town from the Goodson house and be able to figure out my movements because of that.

"Anything you like," Alex said. "Just set it inside the office. It'll be safe. We don't have any problems with crime around here."

"Right," I said in a dry voice, but Alex never noticed that. It was horses he cared about most, not people.

I couldn't help noting the irony in his statement, though.

No problem with crime. Right. Two guys dead already—if you wanted to count the one that I knew about but nobody else did—and there was no problem with crime. Assassins creeping around in the bushes and lurking around street corners but, hey, no problems here, no sir.

Oh well. I figured it seemed more of a crime if you were the one being shot at.

I headed for the door.

"You want the brown saddled for you tomorrow?" he called out.

"Dunno yet."

"Whatever." He hadn't once looked up from what he was doing. I wished I could feel so secure in my surroundings as that.

But then it had been an awful lot of years since I'd been able to completely let the barriers down.

You'd think a body would get used to it eventually. I hadn't. Not really.

I carried the carbine along with me, figuring Alex's opinions of the level of crime would be best taken with a grain of salt even if there weren't murderers and would-be murderers in the neighborhood, and headed for the county building.

Sheriff Frake was in his office. Alone this time.

"Alex said you were looking for me earlier this morning."

"That's right, I was, I . . ." He stopped, scratched his head, grinned a little. "D'you know something? I can't for the life of me remember now what it was I wanted to ask of you."

"Huh. Something like that's never happened to me, Sheriff. Not my whole life long." I paused for half a second. "And if you believe that . . ."

Frake chuckled. Then shrugged. "It'll come to me."

"Right after I walk out that door, prob'ly."

"Probably," he agreed. "Coffee?"

"No, thanks."

"Alex tells me you rode out east to those old tumbledown farms. At least he said those're what you were asking directions to. Anything I can help with?"

"Not really." I explained to him the reason I'd asked the way to them.

"You were going to set an ambush for the ambushers? Clever."

"Might've been if it'd worked," I answered. "Didn't work though."

"Next time."

"Sure." I waved a good-bye and stepped out of his office, across the hallway and through a door that had "County Clerk, Clerk of Circuit Court, Tax Collector, Tax Assessor" and "Office of the County Commissioners" all crowded onto a panel of frosted glass in it.

I don't know how many hats the guy was supposed to wear among those, but there was only one man in that office. He was a tall and lanky fellow wearing sleeve garters, a green eyeshade and with an ink stain on the fingers of his right hand. Busy fella, I presumed. He looked up when I entered.

"Marshal Tanner," he said. I sure was becoming well known around town. I didn't recall ever meeting this particular gentleman before.

"I'm sorry. Your name is, uh . . ."

"Nalon," he said. "Clifford Nalon. We haven't actually met, so don't apologize. And don't be surprised that everybody knows you by now."

"No, I reckon I couldn't claim now to be anybody but Riley Tanner, could I?"

"Not hardly," he agreed, not even close to getting the kick out of that that I did. "What can I help you with, Marshal?"

"I was curious about some farms that sold over this past year or so. Loncallo is one of them. Benjamin. A bunch of others."

"Sure, I remember. I recorded the transfer of ownership personally in each of those."

"What can you tell me about them?"

"Is there anything wrong with those sales, Marshal?"

"Not that I know about," I admitted. "Just curiosity, that's all." Which was pretty much the truth. The rest of it was that I could see the same thing coming soon to Bob

Whitworth and his family, and I liked those people. That made me wonder. I didn't think for a minute there would be anything I could do to help them. But the county records were right here practically under my nose anyway, and like I told the man. I was curious.

"Of course it isn't any of my business anyhow, Marshal. Those are all public records. Anybody is entitled to see them even if they aren't official U.S. marshals."

"Just a deputy," I corrected. "Just a deputy."

"That's plenty official enough for me. Any record in this office, you're welcome to see it, Marshal. Including the things the public wouldn't generally be allowed."

I didn't bother asking what sort of records those might be. But then I've never been all that cozy with the law and lawyers and officialdom.

"Just one second, Marshal, and I'll get out my plat book. Will that do to start with?"

"Sure thing." I had no idea in the world what a plat book was. But I didn't want to tell him that, did I?

My new friend Cliff—everybody was my friend here, it seemed; almost everybody—went over to a set of study shelves and brought down a huge, canvas-bound folio sort of thing that he lugged over to the counter where I was standing and laid out between us. He opened it wide, found the page he wanted—the book turned out to contain maps— then turned the big ledger around so I could look at it right-side-to. "These are the first farms sold," he said, pointing.

There were three of them. "Uh huh." I didn't have the least idea what I was looking at. The names of roads and washes and dry creek beds would mean something to the locals but not to me. "Is that all of them?"

"Good Lord, no. These were just the first. Then there are these." He flipped the page over, and I could see three more. "And these." Three more. "These." Just one on that page. "Then," he turned several pages this time, and I could see a bunch of small lots and blocks laid out on the map and guessed that this part would be where the town lots were recorded, "then over here on this side again for . . . let me look . . . this one and the next four pages."

"That's an awful lot of farms," I said.

"Fourteen in all," he agreed.

"They were all bought by the same buyer?"

"That's right. All by the Broad Valley Land and Cattle Company."

"Land and cattle," I repeated.

"That's right."

"They say what they wanted the farms for that they'd buy them up like that?"

"They haven't said a word to me about anything," Nalon told me. "I don't even know who they are."

"You don't . . . in a town this size?"

"The purchases were handled through an attorney, Marshal. A gentleman from Austin. Whenever there is business to be conducted or documents to be recorded, Mr. Hansford comes here from Austin. He has a power of attorney from the board of the Broad Valley Land and Cattle Company."

"You didn't notice who signed the paper for him?"

"To tell you the truth, I looked. But I couldn't make out the signature. Nor did I have any reason to suspect his power of attorney might be false. After all, the sellers of those properties accompanied the gentleman to the closings. I myself witnessed their signatures."

"Fourteen farms," I mused.

"That's right."

"Funny how they're all laid out straight as a string in your book," I said.

"That's because they all lie in a straight line on the ground," Nalon said. He frowned. "I never particularly noticed that before, but it is true. They all lie on an east-west axis more or less."

"That mean anything to you?" I asked him.

"No."

"Not to me neither." I smiled and shrugged. "Anything odd about those sales that you can think of?"

"Not really," he said.

"Any idea why so many farmers might've failed, kind of all of them together like that?"

"No, I don't. The weather has been fine. My wife's garden is flourishing. I would have thought farm crops would be doing well too under the same conditions."

"Yeah, a guy would think that, wouldn't he. Oh, well. It's too deep for the likes of me."

"Is there anything else you would like to see, Marshal?"

"No, Mr. Nalon, not a thing. But I thank you. You've been a big help."

Which was gilding the lily, of course. He'd tried to be helpful, that much was true. Pleasant and open and agreeable. I just didn't see that what he had to show me accomplished much of anything, though.

I gave the man a cheerful good day and went outside.

There were two gents out there, one standing on either end of the board sidewalk in front of the county building.

They had it in mind to shoot me down in a crossfire, they did.

SIXTY-FOUR

I noticed the one on my right as I walked out the door, and about the same time that I caught sight of him, I heard the oily snickety-clack of a gun hammer being cocked over to my left.

It didn't take me long to realize what was going on here. About the same amount of time—and for kind of the same reason—that it never seems to take anyone very long to decide that a skillet handle is too hot to hang onto. It's a matter of self-preservation in either event.

I don't at all doubt that if I'd stopped still or tried to reverse direction to duck back inside, I'd be dead now. Or seriously shot up, if not entirely done away with.

Instead, since I was already moving, I threw myself forward off the sidewalk and hit the ground rolling.

The one on my left had a shotgun, damn him, and he let a barrel go so close behind me that I could have sworn I felt the wind of the pellets going by. I don't know as I actually did, but if I didn't feel it, then I dang sure imagined it real well.

The other one was still busy trying to cock his pistol—they hadn't been ready when I walked out, so I'd guess they either just got there or were awful stupid; not that I'm complaining about it either way, understand—so I jerked my gun out and let one fly at the man with the shotgun.

I didn't hit him, but the bullet came close enough to make him flinch and jump back. He lost his balance when he did that, which gave me time enough to swing around the other way and shoot his partner.

There wasn't time for taking aim or trying to be delicate about any of this, and my bullet hit the man in a place where no man ever ought to be shot.

That did disinterest him in the things that were going on, though.

His pal still had the shotgun and I knew I didn't have time to fool around here. So I rolled over on the ground again to get out of the way just in case there was another load of buck heading in my direction, found my target and squeezed off an aimed shot that took the one with the shotgun square in the belly.

He went white and dropped to his knees, likely knowing from where he was hit that he was a dead man or as good as and that he'd be a lot better off if he could die quick instead of lingering. But then maybe he'd never seen a gutshot man die. I had. It is ugly.

This one, already killed but still breathing, struggled to raise the shotgun and aim the second barrel at me.

I aimed careful and put the guy down. Then turned back to the one who was lying at the mouth of the alley beside the county building. He still had his pistol in hand but I doubt that he knew. Or cared. He didn't present a threat to anybody right now.

I went over to him careful, keeping my revolver aimed about in the middle of the wounded man's forehead just in case he decided to take offense at what I'd done to him. He didn't even see me standing there, I don't think. I kicked the gun out of his hand and stepped back away from him.

About then Sheriff Frake came racing out of the alley from someplace in back of the building, obviously running to see what the shooting was about.

To tell the truth, I was so keyed up and nervous that I like to shot the county sheriff when he busted into view. He had his gun out too and for half a second there things could have come down to a real unfortunate accident between us, because I sure did think he was fixing to shoot.

The good thing is that I recognized him and ducked back against the side of the building and shouted for him to hold his fire.

By then there were other townsfolk popping out of doorways and peering out of windows, and both the sheriff and me were able to recognize that the danger was over.

"Are you all right, Marshal?"

I was shivering and shaking but there weren't any holes in me. I told him that I was and moved real slow and careful while I reloaded my revolver and put it back into the leather where it belonged.

"I don't . . . I stepped outside, and they were standing there, Sheriff. One on either side."

"They had you in a crossfire?"

"They did, Sheriff. I saw them standing there," a fellow who'd come out of a storefront across the street said. "You should have seen it, Sheriff. I swear I never saw the like. Marshal Tanner was quick as a striking snake. Smart too. He jumped out from between them so that one's shot dusted the other one back and gave the marshal time enough to return fire."

I hadn't known that happened. Hadn't seen it at the time, but I guess this fellow did.

"It was something to see, Sheriff. Hickok or Earp or Tilghman, none of them could have handled it better, I tell you. Now I know why you were chosen to wear that badge, Marshal Tanner. I'd sure like to shake the hand of a man who could do something like you just done." And darned if he didn't come over and start pumping my hand. Him first and then some other fellows from among the crowd that was gathering now that the excitement was over.

"What about this one?" someone asked.

"What about him?" Sheriff Frake responded.

"He's still alive."

"He is? I'll be damned."

"We can't take him to the barbershop. Carl is laid up from the shooting that's already done."

"Carry him inside the jail, boys, and lay him on the bunk in that back cell. It's where he'll have to be sooner or later so it might as well be sooner as later."

A couple men volunteered to carry the assassin inside. I wouldn't have. The guy was bleeding something awful. They picked him up, though, and I retrieved his pistol and trailed them inside, Sheriff Frake coming along too.

"Just leave him there," Frake told the men when they put the fellow down on the bare planks of the cot, apparently not wanting to mess up the jail's mattress and blanket with all that blood.

"You aren't going to see to him?" I asked.

"Later. He'll keep."

I thanked the fellows who'd carried the wounded man in, then went back to the cell and looked in on him. He was awake and aware but didn't seem in too much pain yet. Probably still in shock from the bullet, I figured. You see that sometimes. A man gets shot and doesn't hardly feel a thing until the impact of it wears off. Then he feels plenty. I wondered if this guy realized just where it was he'd been hit.

"You doing all right?" I asked him.

"You son of a bitch."

"It isn't nice to talk like that."

"Bastard," he said.

I guess I didn't blame him if he didn't want to be friends. Considering. "Anything I can get you?" I asked.

"A gun, damn you."

"Maybe later. Would you mind telling me first why it is you and your pard were laying for me?"

"Naw, I don't mind. We done it for a hundred dollars."

"Each?"

"Yes, a hundred for each of us." He frowned. "Why'd you ask that?"

"Sometimes a fellow wants to know what he's worth. You know?"

The assassin scowled. I was pretty sure I hadn't seen him before. Not up close. But there was something about him . . . his hat, the way he'd stood or moved back when he still could . . . something . . . that made me think he'd been one of them that killed the real Riley Tanner that day.

"Mind answering one more thing for me?" I asked him.

"What's that?"

"Who was to pay you the hundred?"

His answer was awfully rude.

"I can't do anything like that," I told him. Then grinned. "And neither can you. Not never again, you backshooting, cowardly son of a bitch."

The comments didn't endear me to him.

But then I wasn't expecting them to.

I turned my back on him and went out of the cell.

SIXTY-FIVE

"I hope you know them, Sheriff, because I don't."

"You don't recognize them?"

I shook my head and, without waiting to be invited, helped myself to a seat in front of Frake's desk. I needed one. My legs were limp as cooked cabbage. "I could stand some of that coffee that you offered a while back," I told him.

"With a little something extra in it?"

"If you had wings, Sheriff, I'd think you were an angel come down to earth with just such as that in mind."

He took up two cups and poured them not quite full, then topped them off with something from a pint bottle that had found its way into his desk drawer.

The coffee gave me one kind of warmth, the liquor another. Both felt almighty good when they landed inside my belly and seeped outward from there.

I felt considerable better after a couple sips of the sheriff's special sort of coffee.

"What can you tell me about those men, Sheriff?"

"The dead one is . . . I suppose I should say was . . . Pete Landers. The one back there who wishes he was dead is Thomas Powell but everyone calls him Smitty. God knows why."

"You know them both," I observed.

"I should say so. I've had both of them as overnight guests often enough."

"Locals," I said.

"Cowhands. They've drifted in from someplace and eventually would have drifted on to some other place, I suppose, but they've both been around here for, oh, five years or more, I'd guess. I've been in office that long, and I know they were already here when I pinned on my badge. Landers was one of my very first customers in the cells here. Him and some other boys. Drunk and disorderly."

"Any serious law trouble before now?"

Frake shook his head. "Not really. Smitty, Thomas Powell that is, beat up a man once, bad enough for charges. The victim reconsidered and refused to testify afterward. I had my suspicions about why he changed his story, but I couldn't prove anything about it. I had to let Smitty go with only the week or so he'd already spent in jail." He took a swallow of the good coffee, got up and freshened both our cups. I didn't tell the man no.

"Will you want to take Smitty in on federal charges, Marshal? Or shall we handle the prosecution here?"

I blinked. That was something I hadn't actually thought about right up until this very moment. Charges. Law charges. And me to press them. Lordy, what a strange thought.

Of course I hadn't the least idea how a body would go about doing a thing like that. And dang sure did not intend to ask anybody here in Broad Valley.

"We'll wait and see," I temporized. "Bad as Powell is wounded it might be better to just handle things here instead of hauling him all the way down to Austin with all the extra bother and expense."

"We don't have to decide immediately. I'll leave my paperwork open on the subject."

"That sounds fine to me." I was glad that so far it was Frake and not me who'd been in charge of the clerical stuff. That was another aspect of lawing that I'd never known anything about. Nor wanted to.

"You say they worked as cowhands?" I asked after another swallow of that fine coffee.

Frake nodded. "At the Diamond T. Come to think of it, they've both been riding for Tolliver the whole time I remember them being here. I can't recall another outfit that they've been on."

"Tolliver?" I asked. "You mean they worked for the mayor?"

"No, no. The mayor is George. The Diamond T is owned by his brother Jesse."

"This Diamond T. Where is it?" I couldn't help wondering if it was out east too. Like, out where those farms were going bust. And out in the direction where the true Riley Tanner was run down and killed.

"West," Frake said, blowing that thought to tiny little pieces. "West and a bit north of west. Pretty good-size outfit. It and the Rocker M take up pretty much of everything north and west of the town. There are some smaller outfits south and a bunch of farms to the east."

"I wonder if Jesse Tolliver could tell me anything about why two of his riders would want me dead."

"It's a question I know I would ask if I was in your boots," the sheriff said. "Of course Jesse probably wouldn't know much about his hired hands. Certainly wouldn't know what kind of trouble they might have had in the far-back past. They both could have been wanted for something and been afraid you would find them out, you being federal and all that. They'd know they wouldn't have to worry about me. Not unless there were posters still out on them from all that time back. And as it happens I didn't inherit anything like that from the fellow who was sheriff here before me." Frake chuckled. "The old scoundrel. He got his feelings hurt when he lost the election. Cleaned the place out, files, guns, keys and everything, and took off in the middle of the night the day before I was supposed to be sworn in. Far as I know nobody around here has heard from him since."

"Nice guy," I said.

"Even in the law, Marshal, you now and then are going to find an apple that's starting to go bad."

I figured Sheriff Herb Frake didn't know the half of it

when it came to that subject. But I sure wasn't going to enlighten him.

I finished my coffee and went down to the livery to get old ugly. And some directions out to the Diamond T.

I was almost all the way out there to it when I remembered—too late—that I'd promised Sarah faithfully to be at the house in time for lunch. I figured if I turned ugly around and beat on him some, I could get him back to town not more than a couple hours late.

Instead, not real happy about it but resigned to facing the facts of the matter and hurting Sarah's feelings no matter what I did at this point, I just kept on going.

It didn't seem to make much sense to do otherwise. But I surely did feel bad about it.

SIXTY-SIX

Jesse Tolliver was nice enough, I suppose, but I couldn't claim that he was helpful. He answered the questions I put to him, claimed he didn't know any reason why two of his employees would be interested in backshooting as a sport and made it clear that he had his own fish to fry and it would please him if I took my interruptions off to someone else who might enjoy them more.

I thanked him—for not very much, but then what do I know about lawing and detecting and stuff like that—and headed back toward town.

I wasn't sure about it but along the way got the idea that I was being shadowed by somebody riding fairly far out to the north of the road.

Now, I have been chased more than once or twice, and I've been trailed about as often as I've been chased, and even though I wasn't certain sure about this, I learned a long time ago that it's better to run from a shadow than to mosey along and ignore a threat that you aren't sure about.

And this day I was riding old ugly and not that no-bottom gray horse.

Without question there are horses in this world that can catch up with ugly. Maybe there's lots of them. The good thing is that I've never come across any such animal and if I did would sure try to buy him.

Whatever my maybe-there/maybe-not shadow was riding, he didn't have a chance when I was up on ugly, and well before I hit the outskirts of Broad Valley, I'd lost the prickle at the back of my neck that'd been claiming I was being followed.

I returned ugly to the livery. Hard as I'd used him, he had only a light, healthy slick of sweat on him and his breathing was deep and regular. That horse has nostrils big as buckets, which is one of the things that makes him so ugly to look at, and I suspect a good fifty percent of his body cavity must be occupied by lungs. The workout he'd just gotten would have had most horses, Tanner's gray for instance, staggering, but for ugly it hadn't been much more than a Sunday gallop through the woods.

"Found Jesse, did you?" Alex asked as he took ugly and began methodically and lovingly grooming him.

"Sure did, thanks to you. Doesn't look much like his brother, does he?"

"Huh. They neither one of them look like Beelzebub, but I'd say they're all related."

"You didn't vote for His Honor the Lord High Mayor?" I asked.

"If you mean did I vote to elect George, I damn sure did not. I went to school with those boys. Didn't like them then. Don't like them now. You wouldn't neither if you had to do business with them."

"You do business with a ranch? I wouldn't have thought you'd need stock on that regular a basis to have to worry about that."

"Didn't mean Jesse. Though he's no damn good either. I meant George."

"Apart from all the hard work involved in mayoring, just what is it that George Tolliver does for a living?"

"Son of a bitch is the feed and grain dealer. Only one for a long ways around. It's terrible the prices he charges. Mind now, he won't pay anything when he's buying. But he's real proud of his product when it comes time to sell."

"Buying cheap and selling dear, that's what business is all about, isn't it?" I asked.

Alex snorted. So did ugly. I wondered if I should start

getting jealous, if ugly was taking such a shine to Alex that he wouldn't give the last bit of effort for me any more the way he'd always done before. "Not so bad as George does. They're in cahoots, I tell you. That whole damn family."

"George and Jesse, you mean."

"Yes, them, and their cousin over at the bank."

"Brainard?"

"That's right. They're first cousins. Same as peas in a pod. Not one of them worth a damn."

I didn't argue with him. I'd met all three, and while I wasn't especially crazy about Jesse, at least he'd been civil to me. His brother and cousin had been cooperative and nice as they could be.

"Do you need me to sign anything more? You know. To keep your paperwork up to date?"

"Naw, the one will cover you for as long as you're here."

"Then if you'll excuse me, I have some apologies to go and make." I sighed and shook my head. "I forgot a lunch date."

"With that Sarah Goodson?"

"Is it that obvious?"

Alex laughed. "Son, that is one extra pretty girl. Every bachelor in this county . . . and half the married men too if they'd admit it . . . would admire to share a harness with that filly. Word is, though, they don't have a chance."

"Oh. How's that?" I tried to make it sound like I was asking just casual. You know. To be polite. But I wasn't.

Alex laughed again and winked at me. "The women in town, they're saying Sarah already has her cap set."

I knew better than to ask. After all, if you cut yourself, you don't go looking for a poke of salt to rub in it. I determined I would not ask. Temptation or no, I wasn't going to ask.

I asked.

"Who?"

Alex grinned and maliciously took his time examining one of ugly's feet. Then he straightened, arched backward a little so as to ease a kink in his spine and said, "You."

Then he bent and made believe he was concentrating on nothing but the horse.

He didn't laugh out loud again, but I could see his shoulders moving and his chest heaving as he tried to keep his hilarity inside.

That was cruel of him, dammit. I hadn't thought Alex a cruel man, but that sure was.

I turned and got the heck out of there before he made fun of me again.

SIXTY-SEVEN

Sarah was sweet and gracious and understanding. Either that or she cared so little about me that she didn't care whether I kept my promises or not. I didn't know which and would have been afraid to find out even if I'd known a way to make the discovery.

In any event she told me it was perfectly all right and not to worry about it. And asked did I think I could actually make it for supper because if so she would lay a place for me.

Not only did I promise to be there, I made sure of it by spending what little was left of the afternoon visiting with Carl. I never once stepped outside the house until supper-time. Dang right I was there for the occasion.

And it was something of an occasion in that Carl was feeling well enough that with a little help from his wife and from me he came to the dining room and sat in his usual place at the head of the table.

After supper I helped Sarah with the dishes so Mrs. Goodson could have some time with her husband in the parlor, where it wouldn't seem so much like a sickroom.

Did I mind drying after Sarah washed? Not hardly.

The family turned in early and so did I. But I would have to admit that I only went to bed early. Sleep came late, my thoughts being filled with the sights and scents of Sarah Goodson.

If only that damned Alex didn't hide claws inside his jokes.

Still, I did get to sleep eventually, and the dawn brought on a whole new day. It has a habit of doing that, y'know.

Carl didn't come out for breakfast, but he said he was feeling all right. He wanted to save up his strength for tomorrow so he could preach.

This time I didn't offer to hang around and do dishes. Among the things I'd been thinking about through the night was that by now Thomas "Smitty" Powell would be hurting. Bad. He might be having some regrets and some anger along with all that misery. And it's been my experience that if one fellow is miserable, he often wants his pals to share the experience with him rather than get off scot-free.

I wanted to get over to the jail and have another try at finding out from Powell who it was that paid him to shoot me. I ate, then excused myself and headed into town at a brisk walk.

I wasn't unmindful, though, that I'd thought I was followed yesterday. And that there'd been three men chasing Tanner that day I first was dealt an unwanted hand in this thing. Three men and I was fairly sure after pondering it that Phylo Barnes hadn't been one of them.

There still could be one assassin out there looking for a chance to take me down.

If there was, he didn't show himself between the Goodson place and the county building.

It was early on a Saturday morning, but the sheriff was in. He wasn't shaved yet—not that so very many men in Broad Valley were right now—and looked rumpled and bleary-eyed, like he'd been up all night or as if something was bothering him pretty bad.

"Are you all right?" I asked.

He shrugged and kept his mouth clamped tight shut. That was all right. He was entitled.

"I'd like to talk with your prisoner again."

"Good luck," he snapped.

"Pardon me?"

"Powell."

"Yes?"

"He's dead."

"Run that one by me one more time, please?"

"Smitty Powell is dead, I'm telling you."

"But I thought . . ."

"It wasn't your shot that killed him," Frake said. "Not outright, it didn't. I'll ask the coroner for a ruling of suicide."

"I don't understand."

"He was all right last night," the sheriff grumbled. "I'd brought Jace Leeman in to help me. He doesn't know human doctoring but he's a marvel with livestock. Between us we got the bleeding stopped and gave Powell some laudanum to take the edge off his pain. He seemed like he was doing all right. Of course there wasn't much left where the bullet hit. Couple scraps of skin, that's about all. He asked about it when we were trying to doctor him." Frake made a sour face and shook his head sadly.

"It's my fault what happened after. I told him what was there. Or rather, what wasn't. I should've lied. I can see that now. But I never thought. I told Powell the truth, and I guess he couldn't live with that. He waited until I was gone to make my rounds of the town doors and alleys. That would have been two, maybe three o'clock this morning. While I was out of the office, he pulled his bandages off and got the wound reopened. He'd bled to death by the time I got back here.

"At least I hope he'd died by then. I didn't go right in to check on him, you see. It was quiet in the back there and I thought he was sleeping, so I didn't look in at him right away. About dawn I got up to add some coal to the fire and put some coffee on to boil. I looked into the cell then. There was blood covering the floor of that cell and half the next one. I still haven't cleaned it up. Powell, he was dead. Had been long enough to start going cold. I can't say for sure when he died. I hope it was while I was out making my night rounds."

I could see how that would upset a man and said so.

"Wish you could go back there and talk to him now,

Marshal, but whatever Smitty Powell knew went and died along with him. I'm sorry about that.''

There was no point in fretting over it now, of course. I mumbled a few platitudes to Frake that he probably didn't take to heart any more than I would have, then went outside.

That turned out to be more pleasant than my visit to the jail had been. Early as it was, Bob Whitworth and his family were in town. I saw the boys playing out front of Horace Yost's mercantile, so I went over to say hello to them.

I found them, Bob and Lucy and young Abby standing at the back of the place looking pleased.

"Riley!" Bob sounded pleased to see me too, as I was to see them with smiles on their faces. "Look here what we just got."

"Good news?"

"I should say so. Can I tell him, Lucy? Do you mind, dear?"

"Of course not. The marshal is a friend."

Bob grinned. "It's a letter, Riley. From a lawyer in the capital.''

"Oh?"

"He's coming by to make an offer on our farm, Riley. A good offer, though. According to this his principals are willing to pay two-fifty an acre. And we hold a little more than the quarter section. At two-fifty, Riley, we can come out with a profit. Not a big one but enough to let us start over on a better farm elsewhere. Down in the hill country, maybe. That's fine land down there. More water than here and good soil. We can buy a place cash on the barrelhead and look to a good future. He says he . . ." Bob looked down at the letter again, and his eyes widened. "Good Lord, Riley, he says he will be coming through the area this month. He intends to stop at our farm sometime late today."

"That's wonderful, Bob. I'm happy for you. Not for Broad Valley. It means the area will be losing more good people. But I'm happy for you and yours."

"Will we still have time to do our shopping?" Abby asked.

"Sure. You and Momma get the things you need. Riley and I will have a smoke outside." Bob grinned and triumphantly held a twist of tobacco aloft. I remembered the awful-smelling stuff he'd been smoking when I was out at their place the other day and couldn't help but be pleased for him.

"It's thanks to you that this is happening," Bob said as we went out onto the porch so he could stoke his pipe.

"I don't see how that could be so."

"I was a little upset with you," he said, "overpaying Lucy like you did. I wouldn't have taken it, you know."

"Of course I know. Whyever d'you think I gave it to your wife."

"Well, I'll thank you for the kindness now, but I'll admit I was peeved to begin with. Still, we needed the money. God knows we did. And that's why we drove in this morning. We hadn't had any coffee in months, and the last real tobacco I had was on Christmas Day. That was my big present, smoking that last pipe. We came in this morning to buy some of the things we haven't been able to afford lately. And that's when Horace gave us this letter."

"From a lawyer name of Hansford?" I asked.

Bob gave me the oddest, slightly awed look. "However would you know a thing like that?"

"Just a wild guess."

"If you don't want to tell me . . ."

I laughed and explained how I'd come to learn the name from Cliff Nalon at the county building. "Hansford is the one who has been representing this Broad Valley Land and Cattle Company in the other sales. It seemed kinda reasonable that he'd be the one behind any offers to you too."

"That's him, all right. H. Harlan Hansford." Bob made a face. "There's something about people who put an initial in front of their names."

"Pretentious," I said.

"Exactly. Anyway, the letterhead is from the law firm of Hansford, Hansford and Bryan. And he says right here that he is acting on behalf of the Broad Valley Land and Cattle Company." Bob paused for a moment to think, then asked, "Who are they?"

"That's exactly what I'd like to find out myself, Bob. Would you mind if I was to ride back to the farm with you this morning so I could have a word with your Mr. Hansford?"

"Lucy and I would be happy for your company under any circumstances, Riley. Of course you're welcome. And you can have dinner with us. A proper one this time." He smiled. "You can even have some of the meat if you like."

I hadn't thought he would've noticed that, but obviously he did.

"The pleasure will be mine," I assured him.

And so it was too.

SIXTY-EIGHT

The Reverend Carl Goodson sat watching through a front window while people rode, drove and walked to church. It wasn't something I'd paid any particular mind to before, my habits not being of a churchgoing inclination in the past, but he told me he could reasonably expect to see just darn near all the decent folks who lived for fifteen, twenty miles around on any given Sunday morning.

"Even more will come today," Elvira Goodson said with a note of pride in her voice. "People know Carl will leave his sickbed to speak to them today, and he is well liked by everyone here."

Which I could sure agree with. And said so. Elvira beamed at the compliment to her husband more than she ever would have if somebody said something nice about her, I'm sure. She was a good woman.

Had a pretty daughter too. I wondered if that accounted for the number of young and unaccompanied men I saw going into the church that morning. Not that a young, single fellow can't take an interest in praying all on his own. That isn't what I'm saying. Not out loud, I wouldn't say that.

Anyway, Carl waited until it was about time for the service to start, then Sarah went over and brought back Horace Yost and Carlton Brainard and the town blacksmith, a man named Joe Clary, all of whom Elvira explained were elders in the congregation. They didn't look all that old to me really, but it wasn't my place to comment so I kept my mouth shut.

Between those three and me on one leg, we put Carl into a rocking chair and picked him up, chair and all, and carried him over to the church and in the back door.

I hadn't ever been up in the altar end of a church before, up there with the pulpit and the choir benches. Hadn't been in any part of very many churches if the truth be known, but I wouldn't have wanted Sarah to know that.

We deposited Carl and his rocker beside the pulpit and left him there. The others walked down into the aisle as natural as you please and found their seats, and the crowd hushed their buzz of chatter and settled down. Pretty soon it was as quiet inside there as . . . well . . . a church.

I stayed up there at the front beside Carl.

"You can go sit down now if you like, Riley," Carl told me.

"Before you get to the sermon you worked all day yesterday on, Carl, there's some speaking I'd like to do myself if you don't mind."

He looked confused. That was okay. Heck, I was scared and I figured one scared-spitless would beat a pair of confused any day.

The thing was, except for when I had a bandanna pulled over my face and a gun in my hand, it wasn't generally my nature to want to call attention to myself.

I'd never my whole life made a public spectacle of myself—unless you wanted to count that time at the school pageant a long while back—and sure never before went in for public speaking.

This did seem like a time to make an exception, though. I'd thought about it and thought about it ever since late last night when I'd got back to the Goodson house, and I figured this right here was my best chance to get done the things that needed doing.

So I took a deep breath and gave Carl a smile that I suspect didn't look as firm and fearless as I might've hoped, then stepped in front of that church congregation and spoke up loud and clear.

SIXTY-NINE

"I'm sorry to bother everybody on a Sunday morning, but there's a reason why I have to do things this way. You see, there's been some awful things going on around here lately. And I've been able to pretty much work out what they are, what the trouble is. The thing I don't know yet is why, but I think by having everybody together like this on a Sunday morning when there's no stores or offices or businesses open, we can work together to get a handle on this and find the records we need so it will all make sense."

It was easier once I got started. A little.

"Now, I'm sure you've all noticed that a whole lot of farms have gone bankrupt or sold out just short of it," I told them. "The truth is, folks, there's a reason for that, and it has nothing to do with those men being poor farmers. Some of them were fine people and good neighbors and top-notch farmers too, but they were playing against a cold deck. They didn't have a chance.

"Every one of them, I noticed, was bought out by the same outfit calling itself the Broad Valley Land and Cattle Company. Does anybody here know who that would be?"

I paused there, but nobody spoke up. Not that I'd expected them to. Most didn't know. The few who did I really did not expect to admit to it.

"There's been fourteen farms come empty recently. By actual count. Isn't that right, Cliff?"

Nalon was toward the back on the left side. He nodded.

"What did you say, Cliff? The others couldn't hear you."

"That's right, Marshal. Fourteen."

"Two of those were bankruptcy foreclosures, right?"

"Well, yes. Yes, they were. But I didn't tell you that, Marshal. I wouldn't want to embarrass folks about that."

"You didn't embarrass your neighbors, Cliff. I'll attest to that for you. I found out about those from somebody else."

Nalon looked relieved. As of course he would. He was county clerk and no one would like or trust him if he went around talking about the things he learned in the line of duty, so to speak.

"Those two foreclosures were bought out at sheriff's auction by the same Broad Valley Land and Cattle Company. Is that right, Cliff? For the sake of those of you who can't see him, Cliff is nodding his head. Those properties were bought out by the land and cattle company. When and where were those auctions held, Cliff?"

"I . . . I don't know, Marshal. Mr. Brainard and Sheriff Frake handled the paperwork for those. All I did was to record the documents."

"I'm pleased to hear you say that, Cliff. I expected it, of course, but I'm pleased to hear it anyway. I like you."

Nalon shifted in his pew. Some others in the church were commencing to look uncomfortable in their seats too, but I suspected their reasons would be a little different from Cliff Nalon's.

"Everybody here knows too that someone has been trying to kill me ever since I got here. Since before I got here actually, but I didn't say anything about that before since I didn't know at the time what the connection was. The thing is, somebody wants me dead.

"And now I'm beginning to understand why. It looks to me like someone has been settling up a perfectly legal way to steal land off honest farmers."

"It was Phylo Barnes who tried to murder you, Mar-

shal," Herb Frake put in from his seat halfway back and
to my right. "I've wondered about that so-called colonel
out at the Rocker M. He could have put his man up to it.
Could have paid those other boys too, Powell and Landers."

"Could have, Sheriff, except you and me both know better. Just like we both know but won't ever prove that Smitty
Powell didn't commit suicide like you claimed. You opened
up that wound and bled him dry of blood when you were
left alone with him Friday night. But don't worry. I don't
expect to ever prove that. Won't have to."

My, but that did cause the buzzing to resume inside the
church. It seemed like everybody was trying to talk all at
once for a little bit there.

And a couple men got up.

I didn't for a minute think they were intending to speak.
"You," I barked. "And you. Sit back down. You aren't
going anywhere. When we do let you go back to your offices, it will be under guard, and you'll open your safes and
hand over whatever records you hold in them. Is that
clear?"

They didn't answer. I didn't really expect them to.

"Just to make sure you understand, we're inside a
church, but by God that won't keep me from dropping any
or each of you with a bullet. That's if you think you can
make it out through that door yonder quicker than my bullet
can. Of course if you want to make the gamble, you go
right ahead an' give 'er a try."

The gentlemen in question resumed their seats.

"What I say we'll find in their private files," I told
everyone, "is all the things that I didn't want to give them
time to hide or destroy. That's why I'm making a nuisance
of myself here this morning, folks, and I apologize for that.
But I couldn't think of a better way to do it. This way we
can keep an eye on everyone until we can gather in the
goods."

"You don't have a search warrant," Carlton Brainard
said. "You need a search warrant or the documents you
seize won't be legal evidence. Without a warrant you can't
search at all."

I'd heard about search warrants, of course, but it wasn't a subject I knew all that much about. You could say that my expertise lies more in the area of pursuit than that of legal writs.

"There will be a circuit judge along by and by to make out a warrant," I said. "It's perfectly fine with me if I slap you all in jail and wait for him to get here. When will that be, Cliff?"

"He, uh, I think the next scheduled docket will be in June, Marshal."

I smiled and thanked him. "I reckon the gents in question could give their consent, of course."

"And I 'reckon.' Marshal, that you could go to Hell," George Tolliver said.

"Watch your mouth, Mr. Mayor. We're in church, you know."

"Who are you talking about, Marshal?" a man in the front row who I didn't know spoke up.

"The officers on the board of the Broad Valley Land and Cattle Company," I told him. "That includes the Tollivers, both Jesse and George, and their cousin Brainard at the bank and the good sheriff there, Mr. Frake. The way I think it happened, George as feed and seed dealer for the area was able to squeeze the farmers two ways. He made them pay dear for their seed or boughten feed, and he paid short when he bought their produce come harvest time. I expect we can prove that too. All we need to do is go over his books and compare his prices with the ones shown in the stack of old newspapers over in Carl Goodson's barbershop. I think you're gonna all be real surprised at the differences.

"Then when things went to tightening down, cousin Carlton at the bank was there to give loans at high interest rates. He knew the borrowers wouldn't ever be able to repay those loans. But then that was the whole idea. Even if somebody had been able to make his payments, George would make sure it wouldn't last. And in the meantime the partners were making a short-term profit off the seed and the grain and interest on the loans.

"That takes care of them. And then there was Frake. As

sheriff he was in charge of conducting the auctions when there were foreclosures. Between him and Brainard they could make sure no one else had a chance to bid on the properties.

"As for Jesse Tolliver, well, I admit that I don't know how he fits into the picture except for providing the gunslingers who were supposed to keep me from getting to the bottom of this. Some of them were his own men. He probably also hired Phylo Barnes as a shooter. Barnes was laid off at the Rocker M and I'd guess went to the Diamond T to look for work. Tolliver would have seen Barnes as a cheap murderer and if anything went wrong, like in fact it did, he prob'ly hoped to direct suspicions onto Colonel Moore, who as a damn yankee wasn't popular around here anyhow."

"But *why*, Marshal? Why would somebody do a thing like that?" Horace Yost asked.

"I can't tell you that, Horace. I just don't know. For right now, though, I'd like some of you gentlemen to give me a hand. We need to round these gents up and take them over to the jail. We'll tuck them away there while we work out the rest of it and do something about search warrants."

"You can't do that, dammit," the sheriff complained. "The cell floors are still covered with blood."

"So are your hands, Sheriff. What I expect you'd best do is prepare to swat a lot of flies."

I didn't have to hurry about pulling my gun. Heck, I was the only person who'd come to church armed, after all.

Which was another pretty good reason to do all this on a bright and sunny Sunday morning, but of course I didn't want to seem the coward by making note of that in public.

SEVENTY

"Good morning. Who're you?"

The man who'd just walked into the sheriff's office stopped and gave me a strange look for about ten very long seconds. Then he came over and offered a hand to shake.

"Thompson," he said. "Deputy Marshal Fred Thompson?" He sounded like I was supposed to know him. Or that Riley Tanner was.

"Oh, sure. Sorry. I, uh, was woolgathering for a moment there."

Marshal Thompson nodded and reached inside his coat for some papers. "Here are the search warrants you asked for."

"That was quick." It was too. Harlan Hansford had offered to carry the request back to Austin with him. That had been less than a week ago.

"No problem." He yawned, stretched, pulled out a slender cigar and took his time about lighting it. "Do you have everything under control here?"

"Pretty much," I allowed. "Most of them were in the church. I brought them in right away, then went out to Jesse Tolliver's place and arrested him too. He's back there in a cell with his brother now. I'd say the only one missing is the fourth gunman. Nobody has admitted to anything, but

he would have been another of Jesse's cowhands. And one
of them turned up missing after word got out about what
had been going on. His name is Elijah Wilcox. Or was
when he left here. He's long gone by now and is sure to've
been carrying a different name before nightfall.''

"Did you put out a want on him?''

I shook my head. "No point. He's small potatoes anyway." Of course Wilcox would've been involved in the
shooting death of the real Riley Tanner. But I didn't think
it a real good idea to mention that to Deputy Thompson.

"That lawyer you sent tells me you didn't know why
your boys would have wanted all the land.''

"That's right.''

"Railroad right-of-way," Thompson said.

"That makes sense, doesn't it. The ground they wanted
was all laid out in a string. Including an awful lot of Diamond T land that they already owned. It all fits now that
you say 'railroad.' Yeah, that makes sense.''

"Do you want to know something really funny?''
Thompson offered.

"Sure, I always like a good joke.''

"This one is better than most. The railroad they wanted
to get right-of-way for? The one they expected would make
them all rich?''

"Uh huh.''

"There wasn't ever going to be a railroad come through
here.''

"Never?''

"Your boys were scammed by some sharp operators out
of Houston, Riley. They were told if they could deliver
right-of-way and a suitable bribe, the railroad would be
diverted in their favor. What they didn't know is that the
whole thing was a scam. They were being robbed of their
bribe money at the same time they were robbing the local
folks of their land to get right-of-way for a railroad that
didn't exist and never was intended to.''

"Now, that is funny.'' I agreed.

"Want to hear something even funnier?''

"You bet.''

"Somehow," Deputy Marshal Fred Thompson drawled,

"it seems to've slipped your mind that the reason you were sent over here to begin with was to tell the officers of the Broad Valley Land and Cattle Company that they were being scammed. Which the Texas Rangers down in Houston learned about and tipped us to, the case being ours because it involved use of the mails to defraud. Now, isn't it a wonder how you would have forgotten that? *Riley?*"

I'm not real often taken at a complete loss for words. This time I was.

The real deputy marshal looked at me for a few seconds like I was some kind of stinkbug caught swimming in his pudding. Then he leaned back in his chair and let himself relax a bit.

"I don't know who you are. You aren't Riley Tanner. That miserable, stupid son of a bitch couldn't have solved a crime like this one or hit a man-sized target with a shotgun if he was standing face-to-face with the suspect. I talked to some townspeople here before I came to see you today. I was pretty sure already that you weren't that backslapping political hack Tanner. No way he could've done what you did here. Though I have to admit you sure look plenty like him. The voice is different, but you look like enough him to be his twin."

"That's what we thought," I said, improvising now that the first shock was wearing off.

"You met him?"

"Sure. On the trail. I was riding south, he was going north."

"North?"

"This was up in the Indian Nations."

"What in the world was he doing up there?"

"He said he was sneaking off from some debts. Me, I was wanting to get away from a bad situation with a man who thought I'd wronged his daughter." It was starting to sound good to me, and I began to warm up to my story. "We talked and he suggested we swap identities. I thought . . . I had no idea it would go all this far."

"Too far," Thompson said. "I'm sorry, but now that I know . . ."

"I can give you a letter of resignation to take back to
Austin with you. Would that help?"

"It would be a start. And if push came to shove, there
wasn't any harm done. You did a better job of it than Tanner could. Besides, if I say anything about this, some lawyer would be looking for technical reasons to disallow the
prosecution. I expect I could keep shut if you can. So long
as you don't think you can go on playing at being a sworn
deputy." Playing? The man thought this here had been
playing? I wondered what he thought of as serious if this
was supposed to be fun.

"You will give me that letter of resignation, right?"

"Right now if you like."

"Then what will you do?" he asked.

"I don't know."

But I did. I surely did know. Just that morning Carl
Goodson and the county commissioners came to me and
asked would I consider resigning from the marshal's service
and taking over as sheriff of Broad County.

Under the circumstances . . .

The truth was that I'd already decided to do it. Even
before Fred Thompson walked in and found me out.

It would mean spending the rest of my life as Riley B.
Tanner.

But it would also mean settling down in the same town
as Sarah Goodson.

Sarah Tanner? I wondered how that would sound.

B. I'd need a middle name to put on the marriage license.
If there ever was such a thing as a marriage license. Bernard. Riley Bernard Tanner. That sounded all right. And
I'd had an Uncle Bernie once. Bernie'd been my favorite
uncle. Yeah, I could handle being Riley Bernard Tanner.

As for going straight . . . maybe that would work out too.
Recent experience apart, I was already learning that county
sheriffs don't get shot at nearly so often as robbers, and
that was kinda nice.

"Mr., uh . . . What is your name, anyway?"

I winked at him. "Riley Tanner. That's the name I'll be putting on the letter of resignation."

And I reached into the sheriff's desk—my desk—for paper, pen and ink to make it all official.

No one knows the American West better.

JACK BALLAS

__THE HARD LAND   0-425-15519-6/$4.99

Jess Sandford knows about life's endless struggle. He's been farming his family's plot for most of his twenty years, making him hard and strong well beyond his age. So when Simon Bauman, the rich, spoiled son of a local horse breeder, opens his mouth once too often, a lifetime of frustration and anger explode from Jess's fists. He leaves Simon for dead, and leaves Tennessee a hunted man.

__GUN BOSS   0-515-11611-4/$4.50

The Old West in all its raw glory.